ALSO BY ANN BEATTIE

Distortions
Chilly Scenes of Winter
Secrets and Surprises
Falling in Place
The Burning House
Love Always

"A PRE-EMINENT WRITER
OF HER GENERATION...

Ann Beattie contemplates life through the sensibilities of educated, upper-middle-class people born soon enough to have been marked and directed by the 1960s and 70s but also late enough not to have suffered the sharpest personal consequences of those times. . . . Beattie's people suffer emotional and moral disconnection in a world that has yet been rather generous to them in material ways."
—THOMAS EDWARDS, *The New York Times Book Review*

"Ann Beattie's new book of stories—*Where You'll Find Me*—is beyond the fine craft and sharp rendering of moments that have marked her fiction. These poetic stories search for real characters in their confusing ambiguity; they are finished and moving views of a world that strikes one immediately as authentic."
—SUSAN SHREVE

"Ann Beattie's eye is shocked while her voice is fatalistic. . . . One reads these tales like a fast-paced mystery that has neither corpse, nor weapon, nor murderer, yet one is sure there has been some sort of horrible crime—which makes Ms. Beattie a very convincing Hercule Poirot."—JOHN CALVIN BATCHELOR

"Ann Beattie possesses a rare technical genius and the best of her work reflects a sense of balance and artistic control analogous to that found in poetry."—KAREN RILE, *San Francisco Chronicle*

"What's new about these stories is their intermittent lyricism, combined with a shift of voice that signals a willingness on the part of the author to risk subjectivity. . . . Ms. Beattie's cameralike accuracy with detail gives way to something a little more personal and poetic, and the result is stories that have the capacity to move as well as persuade us."—MICHIKO KAKUTANI, *The New York Times*

WHERE YOU'LL FIND ME

ME

and
other stories

WHERE YOU'LL FIND ME

and
other stories

ANN BEATTIE

Collier Books
MACMILLAN PUBLISHING COMPANY
NEW YORK

Macmillan Publishing Company
866 Third Avenue, New York, N.Y. 10022
Collier Macmillan Canada, Inc.

The following stories appeared in The New Yorker: "Coney
Island," "Lofty," "Times," and "Heaven on a Summer
Night" copyright © 1983; "In the White Night" and
"Summer People" copyright © 1984; "Janus" copyright
© 1985; "Skeletons" and "Where You'll Find Me" copyright © 1986. "Snow" appeared in Vanity Fair copyright
© 1983. "High School" appeared in the Boston Review
copyright © 1983. "Cards" appeared in Esquire copyright
© 1985. "Taking Hold" appeared in Fiction Network
copyright © 1986 by Ann Beattie. "The Big Outside
World," "When Can I See You Again?" and "Spiritus"
were previously published by Simon & Schuster.

Library of Congress Cataloging-in-Publication Data
Beattie, Ann.
  Where you'll find me and other stories.
  I. Title.
[PS3552.E177W4   1987]   813'.54   87-13463
ISBN 0-02-016560-9

Cover photograph © 1977 by Joel Meyerowitz
Cover design by Lee Wade
First Collier Books Edition 1987

10 9 8 7 6 5 4 3 2 1

Printed in the United States of America

For David Wiegand

CONTENTS

IN
THE WHITE
NIGHT

Don't think about a cow," Matt Brinkley said. "Don't think about a river, don't think about a car, don't think about snow. . . ."

Matt was standing in the doorway, hollering after his guests. His wife, Gaye, gripped his arm and tried to tug him back into the house. The party was over. Carol and Vernon turned to wave goodbye, calling back their thanks, whispering to each other to be careful. The steps were slick with snow; an icy snow had been falling for hours, frozen granules mixed in with lighter stuff, and the instant they moved out from under the protection of the Brinkleys' porch the cold froze the smiles on their faces. The swirls of snow blowing against Carol's skin reminded her—an odd thing to remember on a night like this—of the way sand blew up at the beach, and the scratchy pain it caused.

"Don't think about an apple!" Matt hollered. Vernon turned his head, but he was left smiling at a closed door.

In the small, bright areas under the streetlights, there
seemed for a second to be some logic to all the swirling
snow. If time itself could only freeze, the snowflakes
could become the lacy filigree of a valentine. Carol
frowned. Why had Matt conjured up the image of an
apple? Now she saw an apple where there was no apple,
suspended in midair, transforming the scene in front of
her into a silly surrealist painting.

It was going to snow all night. They had heard that on
the radio, driving to the Brinkleys'. The Don't-Think-
About-Whatever game had started as a joke, something
long in the telling and startling to Vernon, to judge by
his expression as Matt went on and on. When Carol
crossed the room near midnight to tell Vernon that they
should leave, Matt had quickly whispered the rest of his
joke or story—whatever he was saying—into Vernon's ear,
all in a rush. They looked like two children, the one whispering madly and the other with his head bent, but something about the inclination of Vernon's head let you
know that if you bent low enough to see, there would be
a big, wide grin on his face. Vernon and Carol's daughter,
Sharon, and Matt and Gaye's daughter, Becky, had sat
side by side, or kneecap to kneecap, and whispered that
way when they were children—a privacy so rushed that it
obliterated anything else. Carol, remembering that scene
now, could not think of what passed between Sharon and
Becky without thinking of sexual intimacy. Becky, it
turned out, had given the Brinkleys a lot of trouble. She
had run away from home when she was thirteen, and, in
a family-counseling session years later, her parents found
out that she had had an abortion at fifteen. More recently, she had flunked out of college. Now she was working in a bank in Boston and taking a night-school course

in poetry. Poetry or pottery? The apple that reappeared as the windshield wipers slushed snow off the glass metamorphosed for Carol into a red bowl, then again became an apple, which grew rounder as the car came to a stop at the intersection.

She had been weary all day. Anxiety always made her tired. She knew the party would be small (the Brinkleys' friend Mr. Graham had just had his book accepted for publication, and of course much of the evening would be spent talking about that); she had feared that it was going to be a strain for all of them. The Brinkleys had just returned from the Midwest, where they had gone for Gaye's father's funeral. It didn't seem a time to carry through with plans for a party. Carol imagined that not canceling it had been Matt's idea, not Gaye's. She turned toward Vernon now and asked how the Brinkleys had seemed to him. Fine, he said at once. Before he spoke, she knew how he would answer. If people did not argue in front of their friends, they were not having problems; if they did not stumble into walls, they were not drunk. Vernon tried hard to think positively, but he was never impervious to real pain. His reflex was to turn aside something serious with a joke, but he was just as quick to wipe the smile off his face and suddenly put his arm around a person's shoulder. Unlike Matt, he was a warm person, but when people unexpectedly showed him affection it embarrassed him. The same counselor the Brinkleys had seen had told Carol—Vernon refused to see the man, and she found that she did not want to continue without him—that it was possible that Vernon felt uncomfortable with expressions of kindness because he blamed himself for Sharon's death: he couldn't save her, and when people were kind to him now he felt it was undeserved. But

Vernon was the last person who should be punished. She remembered him in the hospital, pretending to misunderstand Sharon when she asked for her barrette, on her bedside table, and picking it up and clipping the little yellow duck into the hair above his own ear. He kept trying to tickle a smile out of her—touching some stuffed animal's button nose to the tip of her nose and then tapping it on her earlobe. At the moment when Sharon died, Vernon had been sitting on her bed (Carol was backed up against the door, for some reason), surrounded by a battlefield of pastel animals.

They passed safely through the last intersection before their house. The car didn't skid until they turned onto their street. Carol's heart thumped hard, once, in the second when she felt the car becoming light, but they came out of the skid easily. He had been driving carefully, and she said nothing, wanting to appear casual about the moment. She asked if Matt had mentioned Becky. No, Vernon said, and he hadn't wanted to bring up a sore subject.

Gaye and Matt had been married for twenty-five years; Carol and Vernon had been married twenty-two. Sometimes Vernon said, quite sincerely, that Matt and Gaye were their alter egos who absorbed and enacted crises, saving the two of them from having to experience such chaos. It frightened Carol to think that some part of him believed that. Who could really believe that there was some way to find protection in this world—or someone who could offer it? What happened happened at random, and one horrible thing hardly precluded the possibility of others happening next. There had been that fancy internist who hospitalized Vernon later in the same spring when Sharon died, and who looked up at him while drawing blood and observed almost offhandedly that it would be an unbearable irony if Vernon also had leukemia. When the test results came back, they showed that Vernon had mononucleosis. There was the time when the Christmas tree caught fire, and she rushed toward the flames, clapping her hands like cymbals, and Vernon pulled her away just in time, before the whole tree became a torch, and she with it. When Hobo, their dog, had to be put to sleep during their vacation in Maine, that awful woman veterinarian, with her cold green eyes, issued the casual death sentence with one manicured hand on the quivering dog's fur and called him "Bobo," as though their dog were like some circus clown.

"Are you crying?" Vernon said. They were inside their house now, in the hallway, and he had just turned toward her, holding out a pink padded coat hanger.

"No," she said. "The wind out there is fierce." She slipped her jacket onto the hanger he held out and went into the downstairs bathroom, where she buried her face in a towel. Eventually, she looked at herself in the mirror. She had pressed the towel hard against her eyes, and for a few seconds she had to blink herself into focus. She was reminded of the kind of camera they had had when Sharon was young. There were two images when you looked through the finder, and you had to make the adjustment yourself so that one superimposed itself upon the other and the figure suddenly leaped into clarity. She patted the towel to her eyes again and held her breath. If she couldn't stop crying, Vernon would make love to her. When she was very sad, he sensed that his instinctive optimism wouldn't work; he became tongue-tied, and when he couldn't talk he would reach for her. Through the years, he had knocked over wineglasses shooting his hand across the table to grab hers. She had found herself suddenly hugged from behind in the bathroom; he would even follow her in there if he suspected that she was going to cry—walk in to grab her without even having bothered to knock.

She opened the door now and turned toward the hall staircase, and then realized—felt it before she saw it, really—that the light was on in the living room.

Vernon lay stretched out on the sofa with his legs crossed; one foot was planted on the floor and his top foot dangled in the air. Even when he was exhausted, he was always careful not to let his shoes touch the sofa. He was very tall, and couldn't stretch out on the sofa without resting his head on the arm. For some reason, he had not hung up her jacket. It was spread like a tent over his head and shoulders, rising and falling with his breathing. She stood still long enough to be sure that he was really asleep, and then came into the room. The sofa was too narrow to curl up on with him. She didn't want to wake him. Neither did she want to go to bed alone. She went back to the hall closet and took out his overcoat—the long, elegant camel's-hair coat he had not worn tonight because he thought it might snow. She slipped off her shoes and went quietly over to where he lay and stretched out on the floor beside the sofa, pulling the big blanket of the coat up high, until the collar touched her lips. Then she drew her legs up into the warmth.

Such odd things happened. Very few days were like the ones before. Here they were, in their own house with four bedrooms, ready to sleep in this peculiar double-decker fashion, in the largest, coldest room of all. What would anyone think?

She knew the answer to that question, of course. A person who didn't know them would mistake this for a drunken collapse, but anyone who was a friend would understand exactly. In time, both of them had learned to stop passing judgment on how they coped with the inevitable sadness that set in, always unexpectedly but so real that it was met with the instant acceptance one gave to a snowfall. In the white night world outside, their daughter might be drifting past like an angel, and she would see this tableau, for the second that she hovered, as a necessary small adjustment.

SNOW

I remember the cold night you brought in a pile of logs and a chipmunk jumped off as you lowered your arms. "What do you think *you're* doing in here?" you said, as it ran through the living room. It went through the library and stopped at the front door as though it knew the house well. This would be difficult for anyone to believe, except perhaps as the subject of a poem. Our first week in the house was spent scraping, finding some of the house's secrets, like wallpaper underneath wallpaper. In the kitchen, a pattern of white-gold trellises supported purple grapes as big and round as Ping-Pong balls. When we painted the walls yellow, I thought of the bits of grape that remained underneath and imagined the vine popping through, the way some plants can tenaciously push through anything. The day of the big snow, when you had to shovel the walk and couldn't find your cap and asked me how to wind a towel so that it would stay on your head—you, in the white towel turban, like a crazy king of the snow. People liked the idea of our being together, leaving the city for the country. So many people visited, and the fireplace made all of them want to tell amazing stories: the child who happened to be standing on the right corner when the door of the ice-cream truck came open and hundreds of Popsicles cascaded out; the man standing on the beach, sand sparkling in the sun, one bit glinting more than the rest, stooping to find a diamond ring. Did they talk about amazing things because they thought we'd turn into one of them? Now I think they probably guessed it wouldn't work. It was as hopeless as giving a child a matched cup and saucer. Remember the night, out on the lawn, knee-deep in snow, chins pointed at the sky as the wind whirled down all that whiteness? It seemed that the world had been turned upside down, and we were looking into an enormous field of Queen Anne's lace. Later, headlights off, our car was the first to ride through the newly fallen snow. The world outside the car looked solarized.

You remember it differently. You remember that the cold settled in stages, that a small curve of light was shaved from the moon night after night, until you were no longer surprised the sky was black, that the chipmunk ran to hide in the dark, not simply to a door that led to its escape. Our visitors told the same stories people always tell. One night, giving me a lesson in storytelling, you said, "Any life will seem dramatic if you omit mention of most of it."

This, then, for drama: I drove back to that house not long ago. It was April, and Allen had died. In spite of all the visitors, Allen, next door, had been the good friend in bad times. I sat with his wife in their living room, looking out the glass doors to the backyard, and there was Allen's pool, still covered with black plastic that had been stretched across it for winter. It had rained, and as the rain fell, the cover collected more and more water until it finally spilled onto the concrete. When I left that day, I drove past what had been our house. Three or four crocus were blooming in the front—just a few dots of white, no field of snow. I felt embarrassed for them. They couldn't compete.

This is a story, told the way you say stories should be told: Somebody grew up, fell in love, and spent a winter with her lover in the country. This, of course, is the barest outline, and futile to discuss. It's as pointless as throwing birdseed on the ground while snow still falls fast. Who expects small things to survive when even the largest get lost? People forget years and remember moments. Seconds and symbols are left to sum things up: the black shroud over the pool. Love, in its shortest form, becomes a word. What I remember about all that time is one winter. The snow. Even now, saying "snow," my lips move so that they kiss the air.

No mention has been made of the snowplow that seemed always to be there, scraping snow off our narrow road—an artery cleared, though neither of us could have said where the heart was.

TAKING HOLD

Oren, sitting in the back seat, realized that his father's lover, Berry, talked the way people on TV talk shows talk. She would listen silently, her right hand lightly clasping her left wrist, eyes a little too wide for comfort, and when the speaker was finished, she would say, "I disagree," and explain why. Sometimes she did this looking straight ahead instead of making eye contact with the person, as if turning her head toward the lens of a camera.

"Or you can give them a party at home," Berry said to Oren's father, Harry, as an afterthought. "Hang black and orange crepe paper, fill bowls with water, and put in apples to bob for—"

"Welcome to 1955," Harry said. "Do you think the party should be staged in the rec room, too?"

"There's nothing old-fashioned about giving a child a party. I don't believe children wouldn't enjoy that as much as going from door to door, getting a lot of candy most of them don't want to begin with."

"I think," Harry said, "that there are still some few people and some few things that can be trusted, and that the real problem is that we are all so full of unnecessary fear that we overreact to the simplest situations. Now go ahead and zing me. Give me the lowdown on poisoned food and child molestation."

"Why don't you let me drive for a while?" Berry said. "You're argumentative because you've been behind the wheel so long."

Oren was keeping out of their What-should-a-child-do-on-Halloween? discussion. He noticed that they had been discussing children more often. He turned up the volume from four to six on the Nylons tape he was listening to through his earphones, leaned back, and closed his eyes.

Oren was nineteen. He was living with his father and Berry because he had flunked out of college at the end of his freshman year and he wanted to spend a year working before he decided what to do about going back to school. The fact that he had flunked out of school hung over everything like a cloud: it was there when he cut the lawn because he had the time to cut it; it was there when he passed by a window of their house in Philadelphia and saw other people walking up the hill or down the hill, returning from work; it was there when Oren passed the peas. In late-night conversations, Oren had heard Berry disagree with his father's insistence that Oren reapply to colleges. She also disagreed with his father's opinion that working at a bookstore was in any way disgraceful. "He's unpacking cartons!" his father had hissed. "He's not ordering books. He's just some flunky, getting paid by the hour." Berry had urged his father to stop measuring a person's worth by how much money they made. Oren was grateful that Berry had gone to his defense. His father had not tried to provoke an argument for a month. He had stopped looking at Oren's cassettes as if he had found a pile of excrement on the furniture. He had stopped moving the flap of whatever book Oren was reading from one page to another when Oren was out of the room.

The other person who had been very good to him was Nancy Niles, who worked at the store. He had even shown her a few of his stories. She was a good reader, and Oren felt that he could trust her judgment. Nancy Niles didn't think that wanting to be a writer was presumptuous. She told him when she didn't like something, or when she wasn't sure she understood what he meant, and she always told him that she was sure he had talent. Just before the weekend she had given him a present: Rilke's *Letters to a Young Poet*. A paper bookmark from the store had been inserted, with a note from Nancy about Rilke's advice on the use of irony. Oren had brought the book with him in the car. He flipped the book open and read: "Irony: don't let yourself be controlled by it, especially during uncreative moments. When you are fully creative, try to use it, as one more way to take hold of life. Used purely, it too is pure, and one needn't be ashamed of it; but if you feel yourself becoming too familiar with it, if you are afraid of this growing familiarity, then turn to great and serious objects, in front of which it becomes small and hopeless."

On the bookmark, Nancy had written, "Does Nancy believe this, or is she being ironic?" There was a drawing of Nancy, labeled GREAT AND SERIOUS. She was holding a piece of paper, above which was written SMALL, HELPLESS IRONY. At the bottom of the bookmark she had written *NANCY'S VICTORY OVER ART*.

Nancy's sister was a superachiever—apparently, the star of her pre-med class—and Nancy's parents were no happier than Harry that their child worked in a bookstore. So he and Nancy had that in common. And a sense of humor (granted, his was more ironic) that they shared. Nancy was taking art courses at night and seeing a psychiatrist three days a week during her lunch hours, though, so he didn't see as much of her as he'd have liked. He usually saw her only once a week for lunch, since she usually met a girl friend her other free lunch hour. He had started to meet her on Wednesdays after her figure-drawing class, at the coffeehouse where the art students hung out. He and Nancy had made love twice: once in the bookstore when the owner went to a funeral and asked them to lock up, and once at Nancy's parents' house. Nancy told him after the second time that she only wanted to be friends. This made him feel ashamed, in some way he couldn't articulate. He couldn't have brought himself to say, the way Berry would, "I disagree." He did disagree, though, but so far he hadn't thought of what to say. He wondered if, for some reason, her psychiatrist had told her to call it off. Or if she was having an affair with the handsome art student who always kept his eye on her at the coffeehouse. He would rather that either situation be true, so that he would not have to consider the possibility that she didn't like him in bed.

Today would be the first time in months that Oren had seen his mother and sister. Three years ago, Joan-

Beth had remarried. Now she lived in northwest Connecticut, in a big clapboard house that had taken on the
shape of a grasshopper after long wings with sliding glass
doors had been added at both sides. Joan-Beth's husband
was eight years younger than she—a weekend real estate
broker, a stock market speculator, a photographer who
took pictures with an automatic focus camera and had
his prints developed at Fotomat. His name was Phillip
Field, and Oren's father said that what he and Joan-Beth
had in common was that they were dabblers and drinkers.
When Harry was particularly condescending toward his
ex-wife and her new husband, Berry pointed out that
each also had in common the responsibility for a dam-
aged child, and that that might well have driven anyone
to "dabbling and drinking." Oren's sister, Diana, had
been hurt in a car accident when she was a baby; she
had only partial use of her right arm, which drooped,
and her right foot turned inward, though the new ankle
brace allowed her to walk almost normally. Phillip's son
was hyperactive. He could not attend school, and was
tutored in one of the grasshopper legs by a woman who
came Monday through Friday.

Although the bronze plaque on the pillar said Heuvell
Farm (named for the river that ran through it), Joan-
Beth had told them the last time they visited that the
neighbors called it Tragedy Field. Her nearest friends
were in New York City, and she could never understand,
having grown up in Kentucky, how Northerners could
be so cold. Though she hardly ever returned to Kentucky,
she spoke of herself increasingly as a Southerner. Even
though she would say that Diana's problems had been
more than Harry could deal with, she presented this not

as a weakness of character but as an example of how a Northerner, born and raised in Massachusetts, would behave.

Oren had rewound the tape, and the Nylons were speeding into high gear as the car rose to the top of the steep driveway, then crested the hill. The Nylons were the perfect soundtrack for his mother's crazy dash toward the car, across the lawn, running so fast she almost stumbled. Her hair, blonder than it had been when she was a young girl, before she had two children and it thinned and darkened, had grown longer as well as lighter. She seemed heavier, too, and even to have grown taller. She had on jeans and a shirt and a vest—some very fashionable vest, putty colored, with the name of the manufacturer sewn over the pocket.

"Oh, this is wonderful!" she said, opening the side door and dipping down to hug Oren. Their heads bumped, and they were tangled in Walkman cords. He felt an earphone pop off and put his hand up to take off his headphones. She kissed the back of his hand. "I'm so glad to see you," she said.

"Jesus, I thought you were going to run into the car while it was still moving," Harry said.

"Don't be so silly. Don't be put off by a little enthusiasm," she said.

Oren didn't hear what else his father muttered, because he had climbed out of the car. His mother reached up and put her hands on each side of his throat. They might have been two cutouts on an old valentine.

"Are you happy?" his mother whispered, moving her hands to his cheeks. She didn't wait for an answer. "How are *you*?" she said, turning to shake Berry's hand. She dipped forward to do it, instead of taking a step closer.

In a large group, his mother always acted like a duck that sailed until it had reason to dip its beak under water.

"How are you?" Joan-Beth said, turning toward Harry, but making no attempt to shake his hand.

"Not bad," he said, pecking her on the cheek.

In the distance, beyond the apple trees, Oren could see Phillip's son and the au pair girl coming out of the woods. The girl was holding a bag or a basket. Timothy pulled on her arm. He began to run circles around her. When Joan-Beth turned to see what Oren was staring at, the circle became a straight line, and Timothy flew toward them, across the field.

"Where's Diana?" Harry said.

"In bed," Joan-Beth said. "She's had the flu all week."

"Hey—have a nice drive? Catch some autumn color?" Phillip said, coming out the front door. He was holding two glasses. He just managed to hand Joan-Beth her bowl-shaped glass filled with white wine before Timothy careened into him and threw his arms around his legs. White wine sloshed onto Phillip's Reeboks.

Oren shook Phillip's hand. He did not like Phillip because he pretended to be a sociable, casual guy when actually it was clear that he disliked all of them.

"Dropped something," Phillip said, bending to pick up the book that had fallen off Oren's lap in the confusion. "Never read anything by Rilke," Phillip said. The name, as he pronounced it, rhymed with milk.

It was an unusually warm day for late October, so they sat on the metal chairs without their pads, on the back terrace, looking out toward the woods. The trees were past their prime but still dotted with yellow-brown and mahogany-colored leaves. Phillip's son, usually a pest, was playing badminton with the au pair. The birdie

stayed in the air: whiff, whiff, whiff. Then the birdie
was at his feet and he was in tears. He looked up, the
actor expecting the audience's reaction.

"You can't win every time, darling!" Joan-Beth hollered. "You are a wonderful badminton player! Go on
and play!"

The look on the au pair's face was indescribable: something between wonder and exhaustion. Timothy continued to cry, and the girl bowed her head and began to
walk toward him. Timothy was looking at the racquet
as if it had betrayed him. "No!" he screamed shrilly. He
ran toward the basement door, under the terrace. Phillip
rattled ice in his drink. The ice bucket was on the wall.
The wine—a half-liter bottle—sat below it on the field-
stone.

"Don't you want to visit Diana?" Joan-Beth said
to Oren. "She misses you so. You're her hero. A few
minutes . . ."

He shook his head no, sipping Coke from a gold can.
"I told you," he said. "I stood in the bedroom doorway
and we talked. If I get the flu, I'll miss work."

"Leave him alone," Harry said. "There's no point in
forcing him to do what he's not inclined to do."

Oren looked at his father. He wondered if he could
later remind Harry that he had said that people should
do what they were inclined to do when the next discussion about applying to colleges came up.

Berry stood at the far side of the terrace. Phillip stood
beside her. "I'm telling you the truth," Oren heard him
say. "Just try to get an Accord that's anything like the
car you're looking for. You say you want a black one,
they say sure, a white one has just been shipped to them.
You want air conditioning, they say that's standard.

Then they hedge and say that so many of them come through with air conditioning that it might as well be standard. That doesn't mean that the white Accord is air conditioned, though. Don't presume that *that's* what they're saying."

Leaves were blowing off the trees. Timothy and the au pair were playing catch, and the boy was chanting: "Daddy, look at me; Daddy, look at me; look, look, look, look, look, look, look . . ."

"See that?" Phillip was saying, pointing his glass toward a corner of the woods. "That dog emerging from the bushes is a quite fine Irish setter that has been doing a lot of damage to our property recently. Twice I have called the police, and do you know what they think the solution is—given that the owner has told me, face to face, that he thinks it's immoral to restrain a dog in the country? To shoot it. The police are so crazy that they think I should take out a gun and put a bullet into the side of that perfectly good dog over there, that is only doing what it knows how to do."

"We should call," Harry said, and for a second Oren thought that his father meant that they should call the police again. Everyone else seemed to understand what he meant instantly, though, and they froze. Only the chanting went on: "Look at me, look at me, look at me, look at me . . ." Timothy was spinning, arms horizontal. The au pair was walking toward him.

Harry stood. "Come on," he said. "Let's do it before you're sloshed."

Joan-Beth rose. She plunged her hands in her vest pockets. "I most certainly am not sloshed, and I am not about to get sloshed," she said. "It is five in the afternoon, and I am having a glass of wine. I see no reason why we can't have a brief family visit, since we were once a family."

"This is a pointless veneer of pleasant socializing," Harry said. "As you're always quick to point out, it's the North we're living in: inhuman, cold, no graciousness . . ."

Oren realized, with surprise, that his father was the one who was sloshed.

"Then go dial her," Joan-Beth said. She looked across the field at the dog, now snorting into a gulley it had dug. She turned back to Harry. "Surely you remember your mother's telephone number?" she said.

They wait for Harry and Joan-Beth's return in silence on the terrace. Timothy has run across the lawn, wanting to get away from the raised voices. The au pair has gone after him. Oren shakes his empty Coke can. Berry gnaws her bottom lip. They are like people outside the operating room, waiting for news. They want good news, of course, but their desire to have the suspense ended produces a palpable ache.

Harry and Joan-Beth are pretending, as they do every year, that they are reconciled, and that the family is well and happy. Harry's mother never makes phone calls. Once a year, on her birthday, they call her. The rest of the time they write their lies in letters, but once a year they get together to speak to her. Harry's mother thinks she has convinced them of the value of the status quo. Following the call, by what is now unspoken agreement, a large check arrives, which Harry and Joan-Beth endorse and split. Phillip's contribution to this is the yearly picture, later to be tucked into Grandma's Christmas card, of Harry, Oren, Diana, and Joan-Beth. Today he has already snapped it, when they first walked onto the terrace. Diana came down from bed, still in her robe, and leaned with the others against the terrace wall. They looked like four reluctant passengers on a ship about to set sail—passengers who were seasick before they began the voyage.

Phillip pours more wine into his glass. The glass drips water from the bottom. He does not add ice. A strong, cooler wind is blowing leaves from the trees.

"From what I've heard about how manipulative she's been all her life, it might please her enough just to imagine this scenario. That might make it worth getting out her pen and her checkbook," Phillip says. He sips his drink. "What's your guess, Oren?"

Oren is sitting on the wall, swinging his legs. "They don't need the money, so I don't know why they do it," he says.

"Price of everything's going up," Phillip says. "I just priced the new Honda Accords. What you used to pay for a Cadillac."

"They might want the money, but they don't need it," Oren says.

"They're doing a number on her, and they're doing a number on each other; that I can understand," Berry says. "What I'm not sure of is why they want to subject us to this."

"To do a number on us," Phillip says.

Berry looks at him.

"Felt like you had to come along, didn't you?" he says.

"If I hadn't agreed, he would have ordered me into the car," she says.

"You would have let him do that?" Oren says.

"Yeah," Berry says. "When he's a tyrant, at least he's

up front about it." She looks off at the woods. "But I wouldn't let anybody force me to go back to school if I didn't want to go," she says.

"So—you and Harry getting married?" Phillip says.

Berry's hand clasps her wrist. "I think that eventually we might get married," she says.

"He hasn't asked yet, huh?"

The dog is digging. The dog's coat is the red clay color of some of the leaves. In the distance, another dog barks. For a second, the Irish setter catches the sound on the wind, then goes back to its frantic digging. Leaves fly down from the trees.

"Taking a long time," Phillip says, getting up to refill Berry's glass. "Hope they're deep into an account of the wonders of family life, and that we shouldn't take this as a bad sign."

Berry takes the glass and looks at Phillip. "Do you really hope for anything nice?" she says. "Or do you just like to make people uncomfortable?"

For a second, as Phillip looks down at her, he seems entirely sober. Then his grin betrays him, and he raises his glass, as if offering a toast. "Where'd you get a name like Berry?" he says.

"You're so interested in everything, aren't you?" Berry says. "I got it from my sister. She couldn't pronounce V's when she was a baby, and she used to stroke my hair and say that her big sister was 'berry pretty.'" She raises her hand, returning Phillip's toast. "So here's to good luck," she says. "May all the pretty girls grow up and meet wonderful men and sit in the sun with them on lovely autumn days."

Phillip smiles. "And if their prettiness doesn't do the

trick, and if sun-dappled days don't do it either, may
money come their way to ease the pain."

On the ride back to Philadelphia, the three of them
are braced not only against each other's tension, but for
the skid that threatens to occur if the car does not
maneuver well over the roads, now slick with a light rain
and another day's accumulation of leaves.

Harry is trying to get Oren or Berry to talk to him.
"Hey," he says, "if I had a swell son like Timothy, he'd
talk to me. If I had a dyed-blonde Southern belle I'd
saved from being alone when she was middle-aged, she'd
talk to me."

No one says anything.

"What was Berry crying about?" Harry says, twisting
his head to look at Oren. He hasn't gotten anywhere in
half an hour of questioning Berry.

"Leave him alone," Berry says, speaking for the first
time, her forehead against the side window. "What's
to be gained from dragging him into our problems?"

When his father defends him, or when Berry defends
him, Oren suddenly realizes, they are actually defending
themselves.

He thinks this will be his starting point for telling
Nancy about things. Then she will find out—as he will,
gradually—that they never recover from this afternoon:
a few days will pass and Berry will leave; Harry will issue
the ultimatum that Oren either apply to colleges or get
out of the house, because he can't tolerate any more
failure. That is how Oren will come to be living with
six other guys in a big, rundown house north of town—
a cold, noisy, strange house that of course no woman

would feel comfortable visiting, so Oren will ask her to please think of a place where they can be alone to make love. He'll be drunk, like his mother and Phillip, when he says it—fearing, of course, that she is having an affair with the handsome art student, and that she meant what she said before about only being friends. But at least he'll say it and, as the expression on her face changes, a sudden surge of crazy optimism will overtake him so that he'll tell her—intending no irony—the thing that had been clear from the first: that for a dog digging up dirt and wagging its tail at the edge of the lawn at dusk, life would take its normal course; that the next day would be the same, and then the day after that, and then another day.

SKELETONS

Usually she was the artist. Today she was the model. She had on sweatpants—both she and Garrett wore medium, although his sweatpants fit her better than they did him, because she did not have his long legs—and a Chinese jacket, plum-colored, patterned with blue octagons, edged in silver thread, that seemed to float among the lavender flowers that were as big as the palm of a hand raised for the high-five. A *frog*, Nancy thought; that was what the piece was called—the near-knot she fingered, the little fastener she never closed.

It was late Saturday afternoon, and, as usual, Nancy Niles was spending the day with Garrett. She had met him in a drawing class she took at night. During the week, he worked in an artists' supply store, but he had the weekends off. Until recently, when the weather turned cold, they had often taken long walks on Saturday or Sunday, and sometimes Kyle Brown—an undergraduate at the University of Pennsylvania, who was the

other tenant in the rooming house Garrett lived in, in a
run-down neighborhood twenty minutes from the cam-
pus—had walked with them. It was Kyle who had told
Garrett about the empty room in the house. His first
week in Philadelphia, Garrett had been in line to pay his
check at a coffee shop when the cashier asked Kyle for
a penny, which he didn't have. Then she looked behind
Kyle to Garrett and said, "Well, would *you* have a
penny?" Leaving, Kyle and Garrett struck up the conversation that had led to Garrett's moving into the
house. And now the cashier's question had become a
running joke. Just that morning, Garrett was outside the
bathroom, and when Kyle came out, wrapped in his
towel, he asked, "Well, got a penny *now?*"

It was easy to amuse Kyle, and he had a lovely smile,
Nancy thought. He once told her that he was the first
member of his family to leave Utah to go to college. It
had strained relations with his parents, but they couldn't
argue with Kyle's insistence that the English department
at Penn was excellent. The landlady's married daughter
had gone to Penn, and Kyle felt sure that had been the
deciding factor in his getting the room. That and the
fact that when the landlady told him where the nearest
Episcopal church was, he told her that he was a Mormon. "At least you have *some* religion," she said. When
she interviewed Garrett and described the neighborhood
and told him where the Episcopal church was, Kyle had
already tipped him; Garrett flipped open a notebook and
wrote down the address.

Now, as Garrett and Nancy sat talking as he sketched
(Garrett cared so much about drawing that Nancy was
sure that he was happy that the weather had turned, so
he had an excuse to stay indoors), Kyle was frying

chicken downstairs. A few minutes earlier, he had looked in on them and stayed to talk. He complained that he was tired of being known as "the Mormon" to the landlady. Not condescendingly, that he could see—she just said it the way a person might use the Latin name for a plant instead of its common one. He showed them a telephone message from his father she had written down, with "MORMON" printed at the top.

Kyle Brown lived on hydroponic tomatoes, Shake 'n Bake chicken, and Pepperidge Farm rolls. On Saturdays, Garrett and Nancy ate with him. They contributed apple cider—smoky, with a smell you could taste; the last pressing of the season—and sometimes turnovers from the corner bakery. Above the sputtering chicken Nancy could hear Kyle singing now, in his strong baritone: "The truth is, I *nev*-er left you . . ."

"Sit still," Garrett said, looking up from his sketchbook. "Don't you know your role in life?"

Nancy cupped her hands below her breasts, turned her head to the side, and pursed her lips.

"Don't do that," he said, throwing the crayon stub. "Don't put yourself down, even as a joke."

"Oh, don't analyze everything so seriously," she said, hopping off the window seat and picking up the conté crayon. She threw it back to him. He caught it one-handed. He was the second person she had ever slept with. The other one, much to her embarrassment now, had been a deliberate experiment.

"Tell your shrink that your actions don't mean anything," he said.

"You hate it that I go to a shrink," she said, watching him bend over the sketchbook again. "Half the world sees a shrink. What are you worried about—that somebody might know something about me you don't know?"

He raised his eyebrows, as he often did when he was concentrating on something in a drawing. "I know a few things he doesn't know," he said.

"It's not a competition," she said.

"*Everything* is a competition. At some very serious, very deep level, every single thing—"

"You already made that joke," she said, sighing.

He stopped drawing and looked over at her in a different way. "I know," he said. "I shouldn't have taken it back. I really do believe that's what exists. One person jockeying for position, another person dodging."

"I can't tell when you're kidding. Now you're kidding, right?"

"No. I'm serious. I just took it back this morning because I could tell I was scaring you."

"Oh. Now are you going to tell me that you're in competition with me?"

"Why do you think I'm kidding?" he said. "It would *kill* me if you got a better grade in any course than I got. And you're so good. When you draw, you make strokes that look as if they were put on the paper with a feather. I'd take your technique away from you if I could. It's just that I know I can't, so I bite my tongue. Really. I envy you so much my heart races. I could never share a studio with you. I wouldn't be able to be in the same room with somebody who can be so patient and so exact at the same time. Compared to you, I might as well be wearing a catcher's mitt when I draw."

Nancy pulled her knees up to her chest and rested her cheek against one of them. She started to laugh.

"Really," he said.

"O.K.—*really*," she said, going poker-faced. "I know, darling Garrett. You really do mean it."

"I do," he said.

She stood up. "Then we don't have to share a studio," she said. "But you can't take it back that you said you wanted to marry me." She rubbed her hands through her hair and let one hand linger to massage her neck. Her body was cold from sitting on the window seat. Clasping her legs, she had realized that the thigh muscles ached.

"Maybe all that envy and anxiety has to be burnt away with constant passion," she said. "I mean—I really, *really* mean that." She smiled. "Really," she said. "Maybe you just want to give in to it—like scratching a mosquito bite until it's so sore you cry."

They were within seconds of touching each other, but just at the moment when she was about to step toward him they heard the old oak stairs creaking beneath Kyle's feet.

"This will come as no surprise to you," Kyle said, standing in the doorway, "but I'm checking to make sure that you know you're invited to dinner. I provide the chicken, sliced tomatoes, and bread—right? You bring dessert and something to drink."

Even in her disappointment, Nancy could smile at him. Of course he knew that he had stumbled into something. Probably he wanted to turn and run back down the stairs. It wasn't easy to be the younger extra person in a threesome. When she raised her head, Garrett caught her eye, and in that moment they both knew how embarrassed Kyle must be. His need for them was never masked as well as he thought. The two of them, clearly

lovers, were forgoing candlelight and deliberately bumped
knees and the intimacy of holding glasses to each other's
lips in order to have dinner with him. Kyle had once told
Nancy, on one of their late-fall walks, that one of his
worst fears had always been that someone might be able
to read his mind. It was clear to her that he had fantasies
about them. At the time, Nancy had tried to pass it off
lightly; she told him that when she was drawing she always sensed the model's bones and muscles, and what
she did was stroke a soft surface over them until a body
took form.

Kyle wanted to stay close to them—meant to stay
close—but time passed, and after they all had moved several times he lost track of them. He knew nothing of
Nancy Niles's life, had no idea that in October, 1985,
she was out trick-or-treating with Garrett and their two-
year-old child, Fraser, who was dressed up as a goblin for
his first real Halloween. A plastic orange pumpkin, lit by
batteries, bobbed in front of her as she walked a few
steps ahead of them. She was dressed in a skeleton costume, but she might have been an angel, beaming salva-
tion into the depths of the mines. Where she lived—
their part of Providence, Rhode Island—was as grim and
dark as an underground labyrinth.

It was ironic that men thought she could lead the way
for them, because Nancy had realized all along that she
had little sense of direction. She felt isolated, angry at
herself for not pursuing her career as an artist, for no
longer being in love. It would have surprised her to know
that in a moment of crisis, late that night, in Warren-
ton, Virginia, when leaves, like shadows on an X ray,
suddenly flew up and obscured his vision and his car

went into a skid, Kyle Brown would see her again, in a vision. *Nancy Niles!* he thought, in that instant of fear and shock. There she was, for a split second—her face, ghostly pale under the gas-station lights, metamorphosed into brightness. In a flash, she was again the embodiment of beauty to him. As his car spun in a widening circle and then came to rest with its back wheels on an embankment, Nancy Niles the skeleton was walking slowly down the sidewalk. Leaves flew past her like footsteps, quickly descending the stairs.

THE
BIG OUTSIDE
WORLD

There's no way it's going to happen," Renee said. "You might as well get the thought out of your head. I go. You stay. That's just the way it is."

The dog looked at the floor. When Renee stopped talking, he looked up and began to beat his tail again. It hit hard against the banister.

"Oh, take him," Tadd said. "Give him a thrill."

"You're supposed to back me up when I make a statement," Renee said. "We'll be bad parents if we don't get it together."

"We're already good parents. We're taking the dog out of the city to a big yard in the country."

"The suburbs. Not the country."

"You're torturing him," Tadd said. "Stay or go."

She picked up the two bags full of clothes for Goodwill and went down the stairs carefully, peering between the bags. She had also gone to Goodwill the day before. She

had taken three cartons of books to the Strand. She had
returned a soup ladle a neighbor loaned them months
ago. Over the past week she had collected enough cartons to transport the plants. They were moving into her
sister's house in Connecticut, to house-sit while she was
in London for a year. What Tadd didn't know was that
her sister was set on reconciling with her husband, who
now lived in England, and that if she did, she would not
be back. What the dog did not know was that he would
be moving in with a cat.

She shifted both bags into one arm and reached into
her coat pocket to see if she had brought the keys. She
had. The dog's chain was also in her pocket. Some
Kleenex. Although she was the one who had instigated
the move, it made her nervous to think about changing
her life so drastically. In private, she cried. There were
tissues under her pillow. She had bought a package for
her handbag.

A man jogged by in black sweatpants and a black
sweatshirt marked #1. Three boys, sucking luminous
green slush out of tubular plastic packages, came laughing around the corner. She passed the laundry and in-
haled the Tide-scented steam. The people who ran the
place began work before she woke up, and were often
still in the store when she returned home to go to bed.
It exhausted her to see other people exhausting themselves in New York. It seemed that the whole city was
only a container for energy. Or perhaps she was just
being pessimistic—trying to justify leaving. She had quit
her job months before she needed to, out of the same
pessimism. In spite of what the doctor said, both she
and Tadd suspected that the long hours and the tension
of the job had been responsible for her miscarriage. The

doctor had told her to wait before trying to conceive again. This made her sad and frustrated. She would have felt worse if the dog's presence hadn't consoled her. At night he would curl up at the foot of the bed and she would stroke his soft fur with her foot and speak quietly to him. The night before, she had suggested to the dog, as she stroked, that he might like a dog brother in the country, and Tadd had turned on his side, seeing nothing funny about it, saying that one dog was enough bother. He had also said—many times recently—that if they never had a child, that would be all right. She didn't believe that. She was thirty-five, and when they married he had said that he wanted three children.

She walked down the street, trying to put all the near-arguments and all the tension out of her mind. The bird-seed had been scattered in the alley behind the Safeway earlier than usual. Pigeons flew up frantically as she approached, but settled down and resumed their pecking before she passed by. One day she had seen boys sprinkling D-Con in with the birdseed. They had laughed and run away. Boys in this neighborhood were always laughing and slugging each other and cupping their hands around cigarettes the way gangsters did in the old movies.

A man in red tennis shoes and a coat bunched up under his arms asked her for money as she waited for the light to change on Eighth Avenue. "I don't have any money," she said. "How come you look better than me if you got no money?" he called after her.

What she did not like about the city was that she was never sure who was needy and who was not. And that while she thought about such things, strangers, passing by, would tell her to smile.

The metal door was pulled halfway down over the

entrance to the Goodwill store. The metal sides were often shut and the center panel slightly lowered, but as she came close she saw that this time it meant that the store was closed. Not for any reason she could think of: it was too early to close; it was open six days a week.

"You want to donate, put them right down," a man with a jack-o'-lantern smile said. He had been leaning against the window of the store next door. "They get them. They pick 'em up," he said. He pointed toward the door with an unlit cigarette. His other hand was a fist. He loosened his fingers and thumbed up a book of matches. He opened the book, struck one, and moved the tip of his cigarette into the flame. "Sure they do," he said. "Push them up against the door."

She wasn't going to carry them home, so she invented a scenario in which the man was right: an employee inside would see the bags, open the door, and take them in. She stepped forward and lowered the bags to the sidewalk, pushing them in toward the door. Someone came up close behind her and she turned, fully expecting that the man was going to offer more advice. She moved back, startled to see a thin black transvestite, who reached into the bag as if she weren't there. "Look at this!" he said, pulling a blue nightgown out of the bag. He had come from nowhere; he might have dropped from the sky, his presence was so sudden. A short man who had been standing to the side dove at the bag too, tossing clothes onto the sidewalk, then snatching them up again as fast as he had thrown them down. He took a lavender quilted robe out of the other bag and swirled it around his shoulders as if it were a cape. It slipped to the cement. The transvestite held up a ruffly blouse—a gift from her in-laws, too silly to wear—and pressed it against his chest with his chin. "I'm beautiful!" the transvestite said. "I'm going to wear this to dinner. Oh, I'm pretty."

She looked away. The clothes were pretty, and when he began tossing them and draping them around his body she blinked at the flashes of color and could remember places she had worn them, whole days and nights that now seemed to be explained by what she had worn. It was a crazy, humiliating moment—as unexpected as a rude guest picking through your laundry hamper to see what kind of underwear you wore. But of course there was nothing she could do. Wrestle for her clothes? Get into an argument? Appeal to the now silent man smoking his cigarette, who never took his eyes away from the scene, even though his face registered nothing?

At Ninth Avenue, fighting tears, she rationalized that at least the clothes pleased someone. Inside the Goodwill store, they might have been sold to people equally silly or crazy. The corner store was suffused with the smell of bananas. That smell hung in the air and mixed with the smell of hot dogs turning on the grill behind the counter. She got a large carton of Tropicana, paid for it, waited for her change, and went outside. She threw away the brown bag and carried the carton. It was cold and waxy and felt good against her palms. Her hands were sore from packing.

The dog was at the top of the landing, doing a little skittering dance as she walked up the stairs.

"Tell him that the big outside world wasn't that much fun," Tadd said. "Make him feel better."

She went to the bedroom doorway, ignoring the dog, who ran circles around her. Tadd had almost finished removing the books from the last shelf. He worked diligently, giving every task his full concentration. She

wished that he wasn't always so capable, so practical.
That he would say what he felt, instead of joking.

"If you'd taken him," Tadd said, "he could have
watched you doing something charitable. It might have
encouraged him to do good deeds. He only thinks about
himself."

"Stop kidding for a minute," she said. "Say something
serious."

"If I stop laughing, I'll cry," he said. "We've got three
rooms to pack before Friday."

She turned and walked into the kitchen, maneuvering
between cartons. She poured a glass of juice and hollered
to ask whether he wanted a glass.

"Yeah," he said. "This dust has really been sticking
in my throat."

She poured a glass for him and slid past the boxes
again. In the bedroom, Tadd was stretched out on the
floor, his head resting against a box he had just sealed.
He stretched his arm up for the glass. "Goodwill," he
said. "Goodwill toward all." He rubbed his hand over
his face. "They used to have those big Goodwill boxes
all over the place," he said. "You remember that? In
supermarket parking lots, outside of schools—all over the
place. I had a girlfriend in high school, and she didn't
want to make out in my car, so we were in this com-
muter lot and there was one of those Goodwill boxes,
overflowing. I got out and pulled out all the stuff and
reached in for more. Piled it up in a mound behind the
box—a mess of shoes and broken dolls—put the soft stuff
on top. It was like falling into confetti. We made out
there, with cars zooming by up on the highway, and the
car radio on for background music."

He was pulling strapping tape across the top of another

carton he had packed that was waiting to be sealed. He pressed the tape down over one side with his thumb, then cut it off the roll with his free hand.

"Was that all you did?" she said.

"That time," he said.

"What about another time?"

He smiled. "Don't tell me you're jealous about something I did when I was a teenager."

Of course she was—because she knew that people and things never really got left behind: you'd be surprised into remembering them; your thoughts would be overturned.

In her pocket, she felt the dog's leash and decided to take him for a walk. If she were a teenager, she might have returned to the crazy circus going on outside the Goodwill store—she might have gone back with her dog, just to frighten them. But by now a lot of time had passed. Something told her that once she left, they had simply decided what they wanted and then had gone away.

CONEY ISLAND

Drew is sitting at the kitchen table in his friend Chester's apartment in Arlington. It's a bright day, and the sun shining through the kitchen curtains, patterned with chickens, gives the chickens an advantage they don't have in real life; backlit, they're luminous. Beautiful.

Drew has been at Chester's for a couple of hours. The light is sharp now, in late afternoon. Between them, on the table, the bottle of Jack Daniel's is half empty. Chester pours another half inch into his glass, wipes the bottle neck with his thumb, licks it. He twirls the cap back on the bottle, like people who replace the cork after they've poured a glass of wine. Chester likes wine; his wife, Holly, converted him, but he knows better than to offer wine to Drew. Holly is in the hospital now, and will be there overnight; his tests for infertility were negative, and now the doctors are doing some kind of minor exploratory surgery on her. Maybe he would have gotten loaded today even if Drew hadn't shown up.

Drew is tapping the salt and pepper shakers together. The shakers are in the shape of penguins. What a sense of humor his friends Ches and Holly have! One penguin looks like a penguin, and the other has on a vest and top hat. Probably they were manufactured as jokes.

Chester's radio needs new batteries. He holds it in his right hand and shakes it with the motion he'd use to shake a cocktail shaker. Earlier, he thought about shaking up some Manhattans, but Drew said he preferred his bourbon straight.

Today, Drew drove across the mountains from Waynesboro to come to his nephew's christening in Arlington. The party afterward was at his mother's. Before the party he had pruned some bushes, fixed the basement door so it wouldn't stick. Afterward, when everyone had gone and his mother was in the bathroom, he used the phone and called his old girlfriend, Charlotte. That was unexpected, even to Drew. The month before, Charlotte married a man who managed a trendy hardware store in some mall outside of Arlington. Drew's mother cut the wedding announcement out of the paper and sent it to him at work, with "Personal" written on the envelope. Now when he has this affair with Charlotte, his secretary will know. What else would a secretary think about a boss getting a letter marked "Personal"?

It's less than an hour until Drew will go to meet Charlotte for a drink. Charlotte Coole, now Charlotte Raybill. Charlotte Coole Raybill, for all Drew knows. Chester has agreed to go along, so that if they're seen people may at least assume it's just some friends having a drink for old times' sake. Everybody knows everybody else's business. A cousin of Drew's, Howard, had a long affair with a married woman when he lived in New York.

It lasted four years. They always met in Grand Central. For years, people hurried around them. Children were tugged past. Religious fanatics held out pamphlets. It was so likely that they'd see somebody one of them knew that of course they never did, and, to their knowledge, nobody ever saw them. They drank at Windows on the World. Who would ever find them there? Howard had a way of telling the story for laughs—the two of them holding each other beside the gate of the Mount Kisco local, kissing until their mouths felt burned, and then, downtown, sitting beside the floor-to-ceiling windows that overlooked Ellis Island, the Statue of Liberty. When Drew was a little boy, he went to New York with his family. They climbed up the statue, and for years he still believed what his father told him—that he'd climbed into the thumb. Howard's lover divorced her husband but married someone else. Howard got bitter and took it out on everybody. Once, he told Drew and Chester that they were nowhere, that they'd never examined anything for a moment in their lives. What did Howard know, Drew thinks. Howard used to look out high windows and he ended up in another skyscraper, in a shrink's office, with the blinds closed.

Drew says, "Charlotte's elbows were pointy, like a hard lemon. I used to hold on to her elbows when I made love to her. What a thing to be sitting here remembering."

"Drew, she's meeting you for a drink," Chester says sadly. "She's not going to leave her husband."

Chester taps the radio lightly on the table, the way he'd tap a cigarette out of a pack. Drew and Chester don't smoke. They haven't smoked since college. Drew met Charlotte and fell in love with her when he was a sophomore in college. "She's a *kid*," Howard had said to him back then, in one of those late-night fraternity-house rap sessions. Howard always took a fatherly tone, although he was only two years ahead of them. "Let's call Howard," Drew says now. "Ask him what he thinks about Holly." Howard is a surgeon in Seattle. They track him down sometimes at the hospital, or through his answering service, late at night. A couple of times, drunk, they disguised their voices and gave garbled panicky accounts of what they thought Howard would recognize as a heart attack or a ruptured appendix.

"I met the doctor Holly's been going to," Chester says. He points at the kitchen ceiling. "If *that* God Almighty and her God Almighty gynecologist think there's no reason why she can't have a baby, I'm just going to wait this one out."

"I just thought we might call him," Drew says. He takes off his shoes.

"No point calling about this," Chester says. Chester pours himself another drink. He rubs his hair back off his forehead, and that feels good. He does it again, then once again.

"Call the hospital and see how she made out," Drew says.

"I'm her husband and you think I wasn't *there*? I saw her. They wheeled her out and she said that she didn't care if she never had a kid—that she couldn't stand to feel like ice. That was the, you know . . . anesthetic. I held her feet in my hands for an hour. She was asleep and the nurse told me to go home. In the morning, when Dr. High and Mighty shows up, I guess we'll know something. How come you're so full of advice?"

"I didn't give any advice. I said to call her," Drew says.

Drew holds the bottle against his forehead for a second, then puts it back on the table. "I'm hungry," he says. "I ought to do everything before I see Charlotte, shouldn't I? Eat so there'll be time to talk. Drink and get sober. Do it all beforehand."

"How come you decided to call Charlotte today?" Chester says.

"My nephew—"

"I mean why call *Charlotte?* Why call her?"

This time, Drew fiddles with the radio, and a station comes in, faintly. They both listen, surprised. It's still only October, and the man is talking about the number of shopping days left until Christmas. Drew moves the dial and loses the station. He can't get it back. He shoves the radio across the table. A penguin tips over. It rests there, with its pointed face on the radio.

"I'll have another drink and stand her up," Drew says.

"Oh, I can do it for you," Chester says, and sets the penguin upright.

"Aren't you a million laughs," Drew says. "*Charlotte—* not the penguin. Charlotte, Charlotte—Charlotte who isn't going to leave her husband. Does that get her name into the conversation enough?"

"I don't want to go with you," Chester says. "I don't see the point of it." He rubs his hands across his forehead again. He cups one hand over his eyes and doesn't say anything else.

Drew puts his hand over his glass. The gesture of a person refusing a refill, but no one's offering. He looks at his hands.

Chester reaches in his shirt pocket. If the missing laundry receipt isn't there or in his wallet, where is it? It has to be somewhere, in some pocket. He puts his index finger in the neck of the bottle. He wiggles it. There is a little pile of salt where the penguin tipped over. Chester pushes the salt into a line, pretends to be holding a straw in his fingers, touches the imaginary straw to the inch of salt, closes off one nostril, inhales with the other as he moves the straw up the line. He smiles more widely.

"Be glad you don't have that problem," Drew says.

"I am," Chester says. "I tell you, I'm glad I don't even remember being gassed when I had my tonsils out when I was a kid. Holly was so cold and sleepy. But not nice sleep—more like she'd been hit."

"She's O.K.," Drew says.

"How do you know?" Chester says. Then he's surprised by how harsh his voice sounds. He smiles. "Sneaking around to see her, the way you make arrangements to see Charlotte?" he says.

"You've got to be kidding," Drew says. "What a sick thing to say."

"I was kidding."

"And no matter what I said now, I couldn't win, could I? If I made out like I'd be crazy to be interested in Holly, you'd be insulted, right?"

"I don't want to talk about this," Chester says. "You go see Charlotte. I'll sit here and have a drink. What do you want me for?"

"I told her you were coming," Drew says. He takes a sip of his drink. "I was thinking about that time we went to Coney Island," he says.

"You told me," Chester says. "You mean years ago, right?"

"I told you about shooting the rifle?"

"Coney Island," Chester sighs. "Have some dogs at

Nathan's, ride that Cyclone or whatever it's called, pop
a few shots and win your girl a prize . . ."

"I told you?"

"Go ahead and tell me," Chester says.

Chester pours two drinks. After Drew's drink is poured,
Drew puts his hand over the glass again.

"You've got about five minutes to tell me, by the way,
unless you're really going to stand her up," Chester says.

"Maybe she'll stand *me* up."

"She won't stand you up."

"O.K.," Drew says. "Charlotte and I went to Coney
Island. Got on those rides that tilt you every which way,
and what do you call that thing with the glass sides that
goes up the pole so you can look out—"

"I've never been to Coney Island," Chester says.

"I was showing her my style," Drew says. "The best
part was later. This guy in the shooting gallery clips the
cardboard card with the star on it to the string, sends it
down to the end of the line, and I start blasting. Did it
three or four times, and there was always some tiny part
of the blue left. The pinpoint of the tip of one triangle.
The middle of the target was this blue star. I was such
a great shot that I was trying to win by shooting out the
star, and the guy finally said to me, "Man, you're trying
to blast that star away. What you do is shoot *around* it,
and the star falls out." Drew looks at Chester through
the circle of his thumb and first finger, drops his hand
to the table. "What you're supposed to do is go around
it, like slipping a knife around a cake pan to get the
cake out." Drew takes a sip of his drink. He says, "My
father never taught me anything."

Chester gets up, drinks the last of his bourbon, puts
the glass in the sink. He looks around his kitchen as if

it were unfamiliar. At one time, it was. Holly had it
painted pastel green while he was at work. Now it's pearl-
colored. Her skin was the color of the kitchen walls when
they wheeled her out of the recovery room. He put his
hands on her feet, for some reason, before she was even
able to speak and tell him that she was cold. Sometimes
in the winter when they're in bed, he reaches down and
gets her feet and tucks them under his legs. Drew met
Holly before he did, fifteen years ago. He went out with
her once, and he didn't even kiss her. Now, when he
comes to dinner every month or so, he kisses her forehead when he comes and when he goes. "I'm persuading
her," Drew sometimes says—or something like that—
when he leaves. "Fifteen years, and I'm still giving her
every opportunity." Holly always blushes. She likes Drew.
She thinks that he drinks too much but that nobody's
perfect. Holly's way of thinking about things has started
to creep into Chester's speech. A minute ago, wasn't he
talking about God Almighty? Holly's the one who seriously believes in God Almighty.

Drew stands beside Chester at the kitchen sink and
splashes water on his face. He's tan and he looks good.
Hair a little shaggy. There's some white in his sideburns.
He wipes his face on the dish towel and swirls water in
his mouth, spits it out. He pours a glass of water and
drinks a few sips. The five minutes were up ten minutes
ago. They go out to the hall and get the keys off the
table. They're on a Jaguar key chain. Chester's car is a
'68 Pontiac.

"Who's driving the Indian?" Chester says.

Drew reaches for the keys. In the elevator, he sees
coronas around the lighted buttons with the floor numbers on them and tosses the keys back to Chester. Ches-

ter almost misses them because his mind is elsewhere.
He has to remember to wash the glasses; he promised
Holly he'd fix the leaking faucet. He'll have one drink
at the bar, say hello to Charlotte, and do some work
around the apartment later. The elevator is going frus-
tratingly slow. If they can have a child and if it's a girl,
Holly wants to name it for a flower: Rose or Lily or
Margy—is that what she thought up? Short for Marigold.

Drew is thinking about what he can say to Charlotte.
They were together for two years. There was a world
between them. How do people make small talk when
they've shared a world? And if you say something real,
it always seems too sudden. There are a lot of things
he'd like to know, questions he could probably shoot out
like gunfire. She really loved him, and she married somebody else? She got tired of trying to convince him that
she loved him? She read in some magazine that people
who've had an unhappy childhood, the way he did, stay
screwed up? He remembers his father: instead of walking him through museums and taking trips to see statues
and to eat in dim taverns with pewter plates, places that
had been standing since the nineteenth century, he could
have done something practical, like teach him to shoot.
Just put your arms outside the kid's, move his fingers
where they should go, line up the rifle and show him how
to sight, tell him how to keep the gun steady, if that
isn't already obvious.

Drew slides into the car, bangs his knee on the side
of the door as he pulls it shut. In another second, Chester
has opened the driver's door and gotten in. But he doesn't
start the car.

"You know, friendship's really what it's all about, isn't
it?" Chester says, clamping his hand on Drew's shoulder.

Drew looks over at him, and Chester looks sad. Drew wonders if Chester is worried about Holly. Or is he just drunk? But that has to wait for a second. What Drew has just realized is that what felt like panic all day is really excitement. A drink with Charlotte—after all this time, he's seeing her again. What he wants to say to Chester is so difficult that he can't bring himself to look him in the eye.

"Ches," Drew says, looking through the windshield, rubbing his hand over his mouth, then resting it on his chin. "Ches—have you ever been in love?"

WHEN CAN
I SEE YOU
AGAIN?

Refusing to share in a Chinese restaurant," Arnie said. "Tony was a jerk, plain and simple."

Martha and Arnie were in his Jeep, going to La Guardia to pick up her sister, who was flying in from Montreal. Arnie was doing this as a favor to Martha. He had never met her sister. It was her sister's plan to stop her training as a paramedic, allow her husband to have custody of their daughter, and move in with her alienated, millionaire lover, who lived in a huge house overlooking the Hudson. At the moment, though, this was not the man being discussed. It was Tony—Martha's ex-lover.

"If you meet him for coffee, you lose ground," Arnie said. "You get a letter and get a little shook up, fine. That's to be expected. But if you call him and let yourself in for it, it becomes your problem."

Arnie shifted. Then he reached over for Martha's foot, resting sideways on her knee. He grabbed her toes and pretended to be shifting again. "Vroooooooom," he said, leaning into the wheel.

"He told me he wouldn't leave his wife. He said that from the beginning. It's my fault that I didn't take him at his word."

"You're dying for some blame, aren't you?" Arnie said. "Why don't you enroll in the Meg Tilley Sincerity and Self-confidence Course?"

Every day, at least once, Arnie managed to work the conversation around to *Agnes of God*. He said it was the most pointless movie he had ever seen, and that seeing it had been one of the worst experiences of his life. Arnie was not known for his moderate opinions.

Arnie was twenty-one—fifteen years younger than Martha. He played lead guitar in a band called Pennies from Hell. Unlikely as it sometimes seemed to her, he was the first man Martha hadn't slept with that she was sure she could love. She felt slightly protective toward him, but actually he often took care of her. Right now, because he planned to go straight to the club after dropping off Martha and her sister at Martha's apartment, his hair was gelled into spikes. The taillights of the car in front of them made Arnie's pale blue eyes glow very brightly. The whole effect made Martha think of a porcupine.

The tape clicked out, and Arnie pulled another out of his jacket pocket and clicked it in. These were home-made tapes, and Martha was by now so familiar with them that she knew that this one, which began with the Big Bopper, would be followed by the voice of Ed Sullivan introducing the Beatles, and then Emmylou Harris, singing "Oh, Las Vegas." It would end with part of "Oxygene." The tapes were labeled "Crazy #1" through

"Crazy #30." Arnie kept them in a vinyl box that was supposed to look like a briefcase.

"*J'aime la musique*," Arnie said, kissing his fingertips. He was speeding, but the light on the radar detector registered nothing. A glass swan he had bought in Atlantic City was glued to the dashboard. It was a prism, and in the day light shot through it and threw colors all over the interior. Sitting in the front seat was like reclining in a Jackson Pollock. Sometimes, on their lunch hour, Martha and Arnie left the office where he was a pasteup man and she was an editor and sat in his car in the garage, eating take-out food and looking at the spots of light. His parking place was by a window, and the light streamed in at noon. If Arnie wanted to take the car out before 6 p.m., there was a five-dollar charge.

"Make me cool, fix me up," Arnie said, shrugging his shoulders. She laughed. "Fixing up" meant that she was to zip and unzip the pockets slanted at various angles on his leather jacket. She reached over and moved one zipper an inch or so closed, pulled open another.

"That's hip," Arnie said, patting his chest. "I'm cool. When I get a million, we blow that place we work in and you become my personal stylist." Arnie cut in front of a limo, saying, "Limos never honk," as he did it. As he pulled into La Guardia, he cursed the layout of the roads. "Meet you in baggage, unless I can't find a place. Then I just keep circling," he said.

As Martha climbed out of the Jeep, Arnie was slamming his palms against the wheel, drowning out Emmylou with a falsetto, "He will ride for-*ever* 'neath the streets of *Bos*-ton. . . ."

Walking into the airport, Martha wondered if she

might be in love with Arnie. She was sure that she
loved that mixture of craziness and dependability. Unlike Tony, who overintellectualized everything when cor-
nered, Arnie would admit vulnerability by making a
self-deprecating joke. The leather jacket was a perfect
prop, and a joke, too. But she always felt a tingle that
went beyond her fingers when she leaned over and
started sliding zippers open and closed. She thought of
what Arnie had said a couple of nights before, in a bar,
when they had one of their evasive discussions of what
was going on between them. "It's Woody Allen's fault,"
he had said, squeezing his bottle of Rolling Rock as if
it were a hand grip. "He had to go and ruin romantic
love for all the rest of us for all time with his goddamn
lobsters."

Martha stopped walking and looked around in her
purse for the envelope on which she had written Jenna's
flight number. She found it, looked at it, and dropped
it back in her purse. She thought that she had shown
admirable restraint in reading the letter she had received
the day before from Tony only once. In it, Tony asked
why they couldn't be friends. He said that he needed to
see her again.

She was following the signs toward the baggage area,
where she had told Jenna she would meet her, when a
boy about twenty—short, rather nondescript, except for
a pockmarked face—stepped in front of her, pulled a hat
out of his jacket pocket, and pulled it on. Fruit that
had been sewn out of cloth tumbled from the crown:
bananas; apples; grapes; watermelon slices. He was hur-
riedly zipping open an artist's portfolio. "These are rep-
resentative of the language of fruit," he said, beginning
to flip through pages of watercolors with calligraphy

below them. "Currants," the boy said, flipping the page. "Currants mean 'Remember me.' " He began to sidestep when Martha quickened her pace. He ran a little ahead of her, turning, the book still open. She looked at him, frowning. Why was she being singled out? What would she have to do to get away from him? "The orange is faithfulness," he said, talking faster. "Gooseberries are probably the most popular. I don't know why. I think because people love something exotic. Gooseberries mean 'I want to see you again.' "

A man hurrying by with a garment bag turned and looked over his shoulder.

"They're not expensive," the boy said. He slammed the case shut. "Oh, hell," he hissed, whipping off his hat and pushing it into his pocket, walking alongside her now. "It's against the law to sell your work in this airport. They want to protect the people from religious cults. In this airport, they think everybody is religious. I'm an agnostic."

Martha looked around her. No one seemed to be coming toward them. She looked the boy straight in the eye. "I'm not buying anything," she said, very slowly and distinctly. "I want you to stop following me."

"Hey," he said, raising the case in the air. "I'm going to tell you something. Did you hear about Howdy Doody? The guy from the show had Howdy Doody in his office, and some people broke in and tore Howdy apart. I got the address of the guy who owned Howdy and for free, I did a big watercolor of every fruit I could think of, and I sent it and said that it was to cheer Howdy up." The boy jutted his chin toward her, and then he turned and stalked away. As he began to move away from her, Martha shuddered.

Outside the baggage area, a woman in a red nylon ESPN jacket, jeans, and patent-leather spike heels threw open her jacket and pulled a young Marine inside. She began kissing him passionately. The Marine carried a duffle bag. He was wearing earphones.

The last week it had suddenly gotten cold, and people were wearing coats and winter jackets. Some were already poking turtle heads out of coiled scarves. It was winter now—she had to face the fact that it was winter—and as she thought about that, the scene in her apartment came back to her: Tony, standing in the living room saying goodbye. "I guess I've just always wanted everything," he said. "I love my wife. Didn't I always say that I loved my wife? You're acting like I stabbed you in the back." He had bought coats at the Goodwill on his way there—three coats that he clutched to his chest so that six dark tweed arms swayed toward the floor like branches bent in the wind. Could he possibly have meant, all along, not only to break it off with her that particular day, but also to have stopped to buy coats on his way to tell her? *Three coats*, she thought—go ahead and indulge yourself and think of it symbolically: whether he realized it or not, Tony was going to be out in the cold, no matter what he did. Because he wasn't going to make it with his wife. If he had fallen in love with her, then some day he would fall in love with someone else. He wasn't going to be able to sustain the status quo. He just wasn't.

The loud sound of the buzzer startled her, and her head jerked up. The baggage belt began to roll. A crowd pushed closer. The buzzer blared again, and the conveyor belt continued to turn. And then, suddenly, he was there again—the pockmarked boy with his portfolio, gesturing wildly to a tall man in a black coat. The man stepped in closer to the boy and made a swatting motion. The woman next to them backed away. People began to clear a space and to stare. From where she stood, Martha could hear only a few words of the argument—it seemed that the man was hissing instead of talking—and then, as he stepped closer to the boy, the boy took a step backward and leaped, and in one second he was steadying himself on the conveyor belt, portfolio clutched to his chest like a shield.

Arnie, who came late to the scene, was the only one to hoot and cheer. *Arnie, Arnie, Arnie*, Martha thought, as he stood at her side. She squeezed his hand and hoped that she could resist ever seeing Tony again. Through tears, she stared at the blank-faced boy, still revolving. By now, of course, the faces around him would have begun to blur; not puzzled individual faces at all: gooseberries on a branch.

LOFTY

K ate could think of nothing but how she had cheated when she and Philip lived in this house. She had put little daubs of glue on the back of peeling wallpaper and pushed it back into place; she had stuffed the big aqua urns at the back door with rags—they were deep enough to hold twenty pounds of earth—and then poured a foot of soil on top. The pansies, pounded deep into the urns by summer rain, had shot up and cascaded over the rims anyway.

The house belonged to Philip's Great-Aunt Beatrice, and she had come in person every month for the rent check, but all Kate's worrying about their tenancy had been for nothing. The woman rarely looked closely at anything; in fact, in winter she often kept her car running in the driveway while she made the call, and wouldn't even come inside for coffee. In the summer she stayed a few minutes to cut roses or peonies to take back to the city. She was a tall old lady, who wore flowered dresses, and by the time she headed for her ancient Cadillac she herself often looked like a gigantic flower in motion, refracted through a kaleidoscope.

In retrospect, Kate realized that the house must have looked perfectly presentable. When she and Philip first moved in and were in love with each other, they were in love with the place, and when they were no longer in love the house seemed to sink in sympathy. The sagging front step made her sad; a shutter fell from the second story one night, frightening them into each other's arms.

When the two of them decided to part, they agreed that it was silly not to stay on until the lease was up at the end of summer. Philip's young daughter was visiting just then, and she was having a wonderful time. The house was three stories high—there was certainly room enough to avoid each other. He was being transferred to Germany by his firm in September. Kate planned to move to New York, and this way she could take her time looking for a place. Wadding newspaper to stuff into the urns for another summer, she had been shocked at how tightly she crushed it—as if by directing her energy into her hands she could fight back tears.

Today, ten years later, Kate was back at the house. Philip's daughter, Monica, was eighteen now, and a friend of Monica's was renting the house. Today was Monica's engagement party. Kate sat in a lawn chair. The lawn was nicely mowed. The ugly urns were gone, and a fuchsia plant hung from the lamppost beside the back door. A fuzz of green spread over a part of the lawn plot that had been newly plowed for a garden. The big maple tree that encroached on the kitchen had grown huge; she wondered if any light could penetrate that room now.

She knew that the spike in the maple tree would still be there. It had been there, mysteriously in place, when they first moved in. She walked up to the tree and put her hand on it. It was rusted, but still the height to allow a person to get a foot up, so that he could pull himself up into the nearest overhead branches.

Before the party, Philip had sent Monica a note that Monica showed to Kate with a sneer. He said that he was not going to attend the celebration of a mistake; she was too young to marry, and he would have nothing to do with the event. Kate thought that his not being there had less to do with his daughter and more to do with Kate and him. Either he still loved her or else he hated her. She closed her hand around the spike in the tree.

"Climb up so I can look up your skirt," her husband said.

And then he was surprised when she did.

Ignoring the finger she'd scraped on the bark pulling herself up, she stood on the first high branch and reached behind to tug her skirt free, laughing and letting the skirt drift away from her body. She went one branch higher, carefully, and leaned out to look down. She turned and leaned against a higher branch, facing him, and raised her skirt.

"O.K.," he said, laughing, too. "Be careful."

She realized that she had never looked down on him before—not out of a window, not in any situation she could think of. She was twelve or fifteen feet off the ground. She went one branch higher. She looked down again and saw him move closer to the tree, as quickly as a magnet. He was smaller.

"Birds used to peck birdseed from a seeded bell that

dangled from there," she said, pointing to the branch
her husband could almost touch. "This tree used to be
filled with birds in the morning. They were so loud that
you could hear them over the bacon sputtering."

"Come down," he said.

She felt a little frightened when she saw how small
his raised hand was. Her body felt light, and she held
on tighter.

"Sweetheart," he said.

A young man in a white jacket was coming toward her
husband, carrying two drinks. "Whoa, up there!" he
called. She smiled down. In a second, a little girl began
to run toward the man. She was about two years old,
and not steady on her feet where the lawn began to slope
and the tree's roots pushed out of the ground. The man
quickly handed the drinks to her husband and turned
to swoop up the child as she stumbled. Kate, braced for
the child's cry, exhaled when nothing happened.

"There used to be a tree house," Kate said. "We hung
paper lanterns from it when we had a party."

"I know," her husband said. He was still reaching up,
a drink in each hand. The man standing with him
frowned. He reclaimed his drink and began to edge away,
talking to the little girl. Her husband put his drink on
the grass.

"Up in the tree!" the little girl squealed. She turned
to look over her shoulder.

"That's right," the man said. "Somebody's up in the
tree."

The glass at her husband's feet had tipped over.

"We didn't," Kate said. "I made it up."

He said, "Shall I come up and get you?" He touched

his hand to the spike. Or else she thought he did; she couldn't lean far enough forward to see.

"You're so nice to me," she said.

He moved back and stretched up his arms.

She had never been daring when she was young, and she wanted to stand her ground now. It made her giddy to realize how odd a thought that was—the contradiction between "standing your ground" and being balanced in a tree. There could have been a tree house. And who else but she and Philip would have lived in such a place and not had lawn parties? She didn't think Monica was wrong about getting married; her fiancé was charming and silly and energetic. Her own husband was very charming—demonstrative only in private, surprised by her pranks to such an extent that she often thought he subtly encouraged her to act up because he admired people who could do such things. He was modest. It wasn't like him to say, "Climb up so I can look up your skirt."

"I'll fly," she said.

He dropped his hands to his sides. "A walk in the woods," he said.

At the back of the lawn, where the lawn tapered into the woods, the man and his daughter were crouched, looking at something in the grass. Kate could hear piano music coming from inside the house.

"A drive," her husband said. "We'll walk out on the celebration for a few minutes."

She shook her head no. Then her ribs felt like a tourniquet, and she decided to start down before she was in more pain. She was embarrassed that there was nothing courageous about her careful, gingerly descent. She felt the sweat above her lip and noticed, for the first time, a streak of blood along the side of her hand—the cut on her finger that had now stopped bleeding. She put her finger to her lips, and the salty taste brought tears to her eyes. She put her feet on the ground and faced her husband, then made the dramatic gesture of raising her arms and fanning them open for a second, as wide as a trellis, before they closed around him.

HIGH SCHOOL

M_y feeling," Liz says, "is that for whatever reason you duck your head and slam on the brakes, it's *mad* to act like that in the Holland Tunnel. Those Jersey punks have been carrying water pistols for years."

"It was a gut response," Matt says.

"And to press the point with the police . . ."

"You have a disproportionate fear of cops, Liz. It isn't Nazi Germany."

"Listen," Liz says, "no cop in his right mind wants to hear what happened in the Holland Tunnel."

Liz is stroking her bangs into place. At the red light, a minute ago, she outlined her lips with red lip pencil and stroked color below her cheekbones. She keeps her cosmetics in a plastic tray that fits between the front seats. It's what other people put their packages of Kleenex in. She flips down the visor and looks at herself. She takes the top off a tube of lipstick and moves closer

to the mirror. I stop looking. Out the right window of
the car, the Hudson is sparkling. I'm in the back seat,
and Hunter, Matt and Liz's four-month-old, is sprawled
across my lap, his head cradled in my arm, my other
hand lightly resting on his stomach. Deep in sleep, he
breathes the way Liz panted through labor. Today will
be the first time Liz has worked since Hunter's birth.
She intended to quit, but she missed working. Not the
modeling, but her pals in the business. I met her a year
and a half ago, when I was a photographer's assistant.
This is the first time I've seen her put on makeup to go
to work; it's probably to make a good impression her
first day back.

Matt keeps looking at Liz. "Hunter," he finally says,
"is your mother at all logical?"

We've turned off the highway, and we're stuck in
traffic, edging our way to the parking garage where Matt's
leaving the car. A man in a hat and coat, in the car next
to ours, looks at me and smacks his lips in a kiss. He
puckers his lips again and slowly moves them open and
closed, like a goldfish. While I'm staring at him, Liz
picks up her bag and throws open the car door. "You're
not going to turn Hunter against me," she says. "Boys
always like their mother." She slams the door and walks
off. Her shoulder bag slips, and everything pours onto
the sidewalk. I look back at the man in the car beside
us. Still making his fish face, he salutes.

Matt knocks three times and opens the door to Coop's
loft with his key. Cooper is Matt's brother. He looks like
a thug, cigarette dangling from his lips, two smudges of
bruise above and below his eye. He's lying on his sofa,
wearing a black sweatshirt and black sweatpants, talking

on his cordless phone. Dom, the cook, stands by his feet. My myopia is getting worse; until we come close, I mistake a bunch of broccoli for a bonsai tree.

Matt helps me off with my sweater, then takes off his jacket. Hunter is in his blue Snuglee, sleeping against Matt's chest. Matt and Coop hold up a hand in greeting. Coop's hand is in a cast. Bracing himself as his car went out of control in the Holland Tunnel last week, he broke his wrist. Dom smiles at us and does a little jack-in-the-box jerk. He had the hiccoughs. Dom hiccoughs again and walks into the kitchen.

"There's no problem with that at all," Coop says into the phone. "Just send me all your receipts through October, so we can close out the corporation." He turns the phone off. "Dom," he hollers. "Why are you walking around with a bunch of broccoli?"

No answer. Coop smiles at his nephew. "How's itsy bitsy spider?" Coop says, changing his voice to a higher register, getting up and patting his good hand on top of Hunter's head.

I give Coop a hug, excuse myself and go into the bathroom. Four gray towels hang on one wall. Above them is a grow light sunk in the ceiling that glows lavender. Pink-budded plants cascade from a shelf above the towels. There's sweat above my top lip. I rub it away, unbutton my shirt and feel the side of my breast. The lump is still there. I stand sideways and look in the mirror, but it doesn't show. I push it lightly, until my skin feels sore. Then I button the shirt again. I'm looking at the photograph hung next to the sink. Although the picture was taken, I presume, when Trigger was alive, his eyes look dead. It's as if he's already been stuffed. Dale Evans stands on one side of Trigger, Roy Rogers on the other. The picture is autographed "For Cooper—Only ride happy trails. Roy Rogers."

I leave the bathroom and go back to the front room.

Matt is settling Hunter in a hammock that stretches between two pillars at the entrance to the part of the loft that is Coop's office.

"Go look at Dom's broccoli," Coop says to me quietly. "He doesn't feel like anybody's interested in what he's doing."

In the kitchen, Dom is chopping vegetables for our lunch. A huge wok sputters on the front burner.

"I'm an artist," Dom says, placing one hand over the other and chopping very fast. "He wouldn't make a painter feel peculiar for admiring a special paintbrush. I try to show him this organically grown broccoli and he acts like I'm peculiar. If I do anything except throw the food in front of him, I'm being excessive. Well, forgive *me* for not being interested in the world of high finance." Dom's part is crooked. He tosses his head left and right as he chops. He's chewing his bottom lip. "You act like you're mute," he says to me. "Sometimes you're very talkative, and other times you come out here and stand around, which would make anyone nervous. If you think I'm wrong in what I say, why don't you just tell me?"

I take the spatula and push broccoli stalks into the garbage disposal. "You're completely wrong," I say.

Dom's face starts to cloud over. Then he smiles. "I'm not going to let you make me mad," he says. "You can all think anything you want, but I know I'm right. I'm at peace with myself." The smile is a smirk. He picks up the chopping board and vegetables rush into the hot oil in the wok. "I cook the best food you've ever eaten," he says. "I make these with tamari, virgin olive oil, and fresh garlic. They're the best vegetables any of you ever ate."

"Stir-fried vegetables aren't exactly unique," I say.

"*These* are unique. These are *perfect,*" he says, stirring madly.

In this way, as usual, lunch gets made.

There is a formal dinner on Sunday night at Coop's loft. One of his friends whom I've never met before is going on to another party afterward, so he's come in a Halloween costume. He sits talking to a pretty woman with her hair in a bun dotted with real white violets. Streaks of white flame from the candles in glass holders are magnified many times by the mirrored tabletop. The white light that shoots across the tabletop looks like machine-gun fire in a comic strip. A man who seems to have no occupation sits to my right. He eats only raw food, and has brought his own. He crunches a bud of cauliflower. If a certain kind of pain had sound, the noise of teeth crunching through cauliflower might represent it. I wonder if it would be okay to call Monte if I find out I'm going to die. Monte is in Canada, with a wife he married six months ago. Their child is the same age as Hunter. Monte is Matt and Coop's cousin. I lived with him for a year, and can't stop thinking about him. He comes to mind when I trip over a crack in the sidewalk, if someone in a store jostles me, if I bend over too suddenly—whenever I jar my body. "Incestuous," my brother in Palo Alto said when I told him about Monte on the telephone. I said that since I wasn't related to any of them, it wasn't that. "I'm trying to guide you," he said. "I don't want to argue semantics." Last week my brother called to say that I'd sold myself into slavery. I explained that since Liz pays me for taking care of Hunter, I wasn't a slave. "I don't care if you come to Thanksgiving or not," he said. It was the first time I knew I had been invited.

The leopard across from me looks exactly like a leopard, except that its paws are folded on the table behind its plate. It raises the wineglass, sips delicately. Its head is smiling widely, so there is no way to tell if it is having a good time. The paws look harmless, like oven mitts thrown on a counter. Its black whiskers are as long as broom straws.

Mr. Malone, Coop's upstairs neighbor, is browsing through Coop's books at the far end of the dining area. Malone is eighty-two. He does very funny imitations of people who assume he's senile. Once they assume this, he gives them a bad time. Later, he imitates them struggling to stay civil as he pretends to be deaf, nervous, forgetful, and frightened. It's like some bizarre version of gestalt, Malone sitting and doing an imitation of himself, then springing up to twitch nervously and avert his eyes, parodying the bank clerk, the store owner, the mailman. The leopard looks at Malone replacing *Clarissa* on the bookshelf, and cocks its head. It cuts a small piece of veal. The whiskers move up and down as it chews. At the head of the table, Coop, in his East Village tuxedo, leans close to a woman who models for the same agency Liz is signed up with and describes, with accompanying gestures, his reaction to having a water pistol held out the window, aimed at his head in the Holland Tunnel.

"I had friends who left New York and went a million miles away," she says. "They bought a farmhouse in Vermont, and when they packed, they must have had roaches in the cartons, because in a week the Vermont place was *crawling* . . ."

A little girl, five or six, bends over Hunter, on Coop's sofa. She sings: "I'm a little teapot short and stout, tilt me over and I pour out." The woman with violets in her hair turns toward the child. "Where did you *ever* hear that?" she says.

"Boric acid," someone says.

In spite of what my brother thinks, people who know each other well rarely mean to hurt. We're all so circumspect that now almost nothing gets said. They're so much a part of me that I forget what being private is: even in their presence, I light one cigarette from another. When Liz has had too many glasses of wine and is sick, I'm there beside her, without a word, in Coop's bathroom. I stroke her back. She throws up in the sink instead of the toilet. I'll get rid of it somehow. She washes her face and sits on the side of the tub, her tiny diamond earrings the only thing shinier than her hair. The door has been closed so long that it's cold inside. I always feel old when I'm not warm. I read somewhere that in Alaska people no longer send their women relatives out to sea on an iceberg to die. Roy and Dale smile into the center of the lens, and Trigger looks blank.

Liz says, "Monte wasn't worth your time. He voted for Nixon. When he was a little boy he wore earmuffs. Nobody else wore earmuffs."

· "Sometimes I think I'm falling in love with Coop," I say. "He's always on top of things. He can get people off the phone in less than a minute."

"You're not in love with Monte or Coop," she says.

She shudders. "We're going to freeze in here, and it won't even be romantic. Only *Vogue* would care about two pretty girls trapped in an ice cave."

In the other room, Hunter's crying reaches a crescendo in the middle of Porter Wagoner and Dolly Parton's duet. "Itsy bitsy—don't go up the wall again," Coop hollers. Gradually Hunter's cries become softer. Liz vomits in the sink. I turn on the water. She raises her head, blinks. I remember my father, from a million miles away, in the land of no roaches, telling me that he was going to pour the contents of my aquarium down the sink if I didn't take care of it properly. I had tried—with childish good intentions—to drop rocks into it. My father told me I couldn't do that: I had to wash them, lower them gently into the tank. I remember what it felt like to put my hand in the bubbling, almost tepid water, carefully lowering one smooth stone after another to the bottom, the little fish darting a fraction of an inch left, then right, and my father's smile of instant approval.

"Porter and Dolly time out there," Liz says. "It could be worse: it could be George and Tammy."

"It could be Mozart," I say.

She straightens up. "The reason I love you is because you really do have a sense of what a big world it is out there."

Dom squirts dishwashing liquid into the sink, stares down as the foam puffs high. He watches as intently as someone watching a roulette wheel spin to a stop.

"I've been accepted into Oxford," he says.

"Are you going?" I say.

"I don't know if I could concentrate anymore. Could

I?" he says. Foam rises, spreads to the edges of the sink. "*Well?*"

"There's a lump in my breast," I say. "All day, I've been trying to remember if a high percentage of lumps are benign or whether they're usually malignant."

"Wait a minute," he says, turning off the water. "You really feel something?" He comes toward me, one hand dry, the other wet. His dry hand is extended. His fingers, separated, look like ribs. "Where?" he says.

I unbutton my shirt, guide his hand to the soreness of the spot. Through his fingers, even, I can feel it; it's almost as large as a marble. We both frown, concentrating.

"It's probably nothing," he says, pulling his hand away. "Go to a doctor."

"I wished it on myself," I say. "A reason to call Monte."

"You think you have the power to form a lump in your breast?"

He rubs his hand across the back of my neck. He pushes hard, as if he's trying to stroke feeling out of his fingers.

"Listen," he says suddenly. "We'll put on some Fifties music and play high school. What do you say?"

I don't say anything.

Dom goes out of the kitchen. In a minute, one of Coop's tapes is playing "Sixteen Candles." It's so heartfelt that sixteen becomes two words, so downbeat that it feels like we're dragging our bodies around the kitchen instead of dancing. Dom's hands slide from my shoulders to the small of my back. My forehead is pushed into his chest and my hands are locked beneath his shoulder blades. We're moving slowly, so perfectly we can't miss a step. He rubs his lips across my hair, his nose touching my ear, nuzzling me. "I'm a great cook," he whispers.

"You're conceited," I tell him.

"Coop couldn't exist without me," Dom says. "He doesn't know anything about California chardonnays. My Crème Anglaise is never too thick. I got Liz from the table to the bathroom so subtly you'd have thought we were doing a box step. Coop knows he can't make a move without me."

"I don't know," I say. My breast throbs. My heart aches.

"You're very good yourself," he says. "When I caught your eye at the table, you knew what you had to do."

I shake my head no.

"It went perfectly," he says.

I shake my head no again.

"Come on," he whispers, moving his hands lower, around my hips. "Come on—you can't quit on me now."

JANUS

The bowl was perfect. Perhaps it was not what you'd select if you faced a shelf of bowls, and not the sort of thing that would inevitably attract a lot of attention at a crafts fair, yet it had real presence. It was as predictably admired as a mutt who has no reason to suspect he might be funny. Just such a dog, in fact, was often brought out (and in) along with the bowl.

Andrea was a real-estate agent, and when she thought that some prospective buyers might be dog lovers, she would drop off her dog at the same time she placed the bowl in the house that was up for sale. She would put a dish of water in the kitchen for Mondo, take his squeaking plastic frog out of her purse and drop it on the floor. He would pounce delightedly, just as he did every day at home, batting around his favorite toy. The bowl usually sat on a coffee table, though recently she had displayed it on top of a pine blanket chest and on a lacquered table. It was once placed on a cherry table beneath a Bonnard still life, where it held its own.

Everyone who has purchased a house or who has wanted to sell a house must be familiar with some of the tricks used to convince a buyer that the house is quite special: a fire in the fireplace in early evening; jonquils in a pitcher on the kitchen counter, where no one ordinarily has space to put flowers; perhaps the slight aroma of spring, made by a single drop of scent vaporizing from a lamp bulb.

The wonderful thing about the bowl, Andrea thought, was that it was both subtle and noticeable—a paradox of a bowl. Its glaze was the color of cream and seemed to glow no matter what light it was placed in. There were a few bits of color in it—tiny geometric flashes—and some of these were tinged with flecks of silver. They were as mysterious as cells seen under a microscope; it was difficult not to study them, because they shimmered, flashing for a split second, and then resumed their shape. Something about the colors and their random placement suggested motion. People who liked country furniture always commented on the bowl, but then it turned out that people who felt comfortable with Biedermeier loved it just as much. But the bowl was not at all ostentatious, or even so noticeable that anyone would suspect that it had been put in place deliberately. They might notice the height of the ceiling on first entering a room, and only when their eye moved down from that, or away from the refraction of sunlight on a pale wall, would they see the bowl. Then they would go immediately to it and comment. Yet they always faltered when they tried to say something. Perhaps it was because they were in the house for a serious reason, not to notice some object.

Once Andrea got a call from a woman who had not put in an offer on a house she had shown her. That bowl, she said—would it be possible to find out where the owners had bought that beautiful bowl? Andrea pretended that she did not know what the woman was referring to. A bowl, somewhere in the house? Oh, on a table under the window. Yes, she would ask, of course. She let a couple of days pass, then called back to say that the bowl had been a present and the people did not know where it had been purchased.

When the bowl was not being taken from house to house, it sat on Andrea's coffee table at home. She didn't keep it carefully wrapped (although she transported it that way, in a box); she kept it on the table, because she liked to see it. It was large enough so that it didn't seem fragile or particularly vulnerable if anyone sideswiped the table or Mondo blundered into it at play. She had asked her husband to please not drop his house key in it. It was meant to be empty.

When her husband first noticed the bowl, he had peered into it and smiled briefly. He always urged her to buy things she liked. In recent years, both of them had acquired many things to make up for all the lean years when they were graduate students, but now that they had been comfortable for quite a while, the pleasure of new possessions dwindled. Her husband had pronounced the bowl "pretty," and he had turned away without picking it up to examine it. He had no more interest in the bowl than she had in his new Leica.

She was sure that the bowl brought her luck. Bids were often put in on houses where she had displayed the bowl. Sometimes the owners, who were always asked to be away or to step outside when the house was being shown, didn't even know that the bowl had been in their house. Once—she could not imagine how—she left it behind, and then she was so afraid that something might have happened to it that she rushed back to the house and sighed with relief when the woman owner opened the door. The bowl, Andrea explained—she had purchased a bowl and set it on the chest for safekeeping while she toured the house with the prospective buyers, and she . . . She felt like rushing past the frowning woman and seizing her bowl. The owner stepped aside, and it was only when Andrea ran to the chest that the lady glanced at her a little strangely. In the few seconds before Andrea picked up the bowl, she realized that the owner must have just seen that it had been perfectly placed, that the sunlight struck the bluer part of it. Her pitcher had been moved to the far side of the chest, and the bowl predominated. All the way home, Andrea wondered how she could have left the bowl behind. It was like leaving a friend at an outing—just walking off. Sometimes there were stories in the paper about families forgetting a child somewhere and driving to the next city. Andrea had only gone a mile down the road before she remembered.

In time, she dreamed of the bowl. Twice, in a waking dream—early in the morning, between sleep and a last nap before rising—she had a clear vision of it. It came into sharp focus and startled her for a moment—the same bowl she looked at every day.

She had a very profitable year selling real estate. Word spread, and she had more clients than she felt comfortable with. She had the foolish thought that if only the bowl were an animate object she could thank it. There

were times when she wanted to talk to her husband about
the bowl. He was a stockbroker, and sometimes told
people that he was fortunate to be married to a woman
who had such a fine aesthetic sense and yet could also
function in the real world. They were a lot alike, really—
they had agreed on that. They were both quiet people—
reflective, slow to make value judgments, but almost
intractable once they had come to a conclusion. They
both liked details, but while ironies attracted her, he
was more impatient and dismissive when matters became
many-sided or unclear. They both knew this, and it was
the kind of thing they could talk about when they were
alone in the car together, coming home from a party or
after a weekend with friends. But she never talked to him
about the bowl. When they were at dinner, exchanging
their news of the day, or while they lay in bed at night
listening to the stereo and murmuring sleepy disconnec-
tions, she was often tempted to come right out and say
that she thought that the bowl in the living room, the
cream-colored bowl, was responsible for her success. But
she didn't say it. She couldn't begin to explain it. Sometimes in the morning, she would look at him and feel
guilty that she had such a constant secret.

Could it be that she had some deeper connection with
the bowl—a relationship of some kind? She corrected her
thinking: how could she imagine such a thing, when she
was a human being and it was a bowl? It was ridiculous.
Just think of how people lived together and loved each
other . . . But was that always so clear, always a relationship? She was confused by these thoughts, but they
remained in her mind. There was something within her
now, something real, that she never talked about.

The bowl was a mystery, even to her. It was frustrating, because her involvement with the bowl contained a steady sense of unrequited good fortune; it would have been easier to respond if some sort of demand were made in return. But that only happened in fairy tales. The bowl was just a bowl. She did not believe that for one second. What she believed was that it was something she loved.

In the past, she had sometimes talked to her husband about a new property she was about to buy or sell— confiding some clever strategy she had devised to persuade owners who seemed ready to sell. Now she stopped doing that, for all her strategies involved the bowl. She became more deliberate with the bowl, and more possessive. She put it in houses only when no one was there, and removed it when she left the house. Instead of just moving a pitcher or a dish, she would remove all the other objects from a table. She had to force herself to handle them carefully, because she didn't really care about them. She just wanted them out of sight.

She wondered how the situation would end. As with a lover, there was no exact scenario of how matters would come to a close. Anxiety became the operative force. It would be irrelevant if the lover rushed into someone else's arms, or wrote her a note and departed to another city. The horror was the possibility of the disappearance. That was what mattered.

She would get up at night and look at the bowl. It never occurred to her that she might break it. She washed and dried it without anxiety, and she moved it often, from coffee table to mahogany corner table or wherever, without fearing an accident. It was clear that she would not be the one who would do anything to the bowl. The bowl was only handled by her, set safely on one surface or another; it was not very likely that anyone would break it. A bowl was a poor conductor of electricity: it would not be hit by lightning. Yet the idea of damage persisted. She did not think beyond that—to what her life would be without the bowl. She only continued to fear that some accident would happen. Why not, in a world where people set plants where they did not belong, so that visitors touring a house would be fooled into thinking that dark corners got sunlight—a world full of tricks?

She had first seen the bowl several years earlier, at a crafts fair she had visited half in secret, with her lover. He had urged her to buy the bowl. She didn't *need* any more things, she told him. But she had been drawn to the bowl, and they had lingered near it. Then she went on to the next booth, and he came up behind her, tapping the rim against her shoulder as she ran her fingers over a wood carving. "You're still insisting that I buy that?" she said. "No," he said. "I bought it for you." He had bought her other things before this—things she liked more, at first—the child's ebony-and-turquoise ring that fitted her little finger; the wooden box, long and thin, beautifully dovetailed, that she used to hold paper clips; the soft gray sweater with a pouch pocket. It was his idea that when he could not be there to hold her hand she could hold her own—clasp her hands inside the lone pocket that stretched across the front. But in time she became more attached to the bowl than to any of his other presents. She tried to talk herself out of it. She owned other things that were more striking or valuable. It wasn't an object whose beauty jumped out at you; a lot of people must have passed it by before the two of them saw it that day.

Her lover had said that she was always too slow to

know what she really loved. Why continue with her life
the way it was? Why be two-faced, he asked her. He had
made the first move toward her. When she would not
decide in his favor, would not change her life and come
to him, he asked her what made her think she could have
it both ways. And then he made the last move and left.
It was a decision meant to break her will, to shatter her
intransigent ideas about honoring previous commitments.

Time passed. Alone in the living room at night, she
often looked at the bowl sitting on the table, still and
safe, unilluminated. In its way, it was perfect: the world
cut in half, deep and smoothly empty. Near the rim, even
in dim light, the eye moved toward one small flash of
blue, a vanishing point on the horizon.

SPIRITUS

The windowsills came low to the ground, and lying in bed, with the pillow doubled over under his head, he could see the lawn outside the rented house. A purple hydrangea was in flower. The window was raised only a foot—his wife hated to be cold when she slept—and through the screen he could hear bees buzzing, though he could not see them without his glasses. He had been fooled into thinking, in the first few seconds when he awoke, that the sound might be in his head—a recurrence of that awful ear infection. Or the nervousness he had experienced on and off for a couple of months, heightening. The last time that feeling went through him—as insistent as the bass turned loud on a drumbeat—he had purposefully poured salt into the wound in the form of going to Spiritus and having a cup of black coffee.

At the beginning of summer, he had resolved to give up coffee.

Today he would walk the two miles to the garage to pick up the car with its new clutch.

His wife slept soundly beside him.

A red towel ("burnt orange," his wife called it) that came with the house was hanging from a peg on the back of the door. His shirt hung next to the towel, and his wife's jeans hung next to that. Her plaid shirt had fallen on the floor.

He preferred to think that it was coincidence—such dissatisfaction, the last summer he was thirty-nine. In September he would be forty. The leaves would be the color of the towel.

He thought of Susan. They had met by accident, then once when she figured out what time he ate lunch in the park, once because he decided not to vary the time, and four times on purpose. The park was across from the new skyscraper—that was where she worked—and one day, walking down a path with him, she had said, "I wonder what the shape of this park is?" She was right; parks of any real size rarely had a discernible shape any more. This one seemed to be a rectangle that turned into a triangle at one end, then bulged into a curve at the other.

He stopped bringing lunch and started going to the stand with her to have a hot dog and a Coke.

He found himself telling her about the bus ride to Fort Holabird for his Army physical; it was more than twenty years ago, yet on the park bench he suddenly felt the rockiness of that long ride again, remembering the way some of them in line had traded gallows humor as they were processed through. There had been some joke about a talking dog in a bar. The punchline had something to do with the fact that the dog had run away from Lyndon Johnson.

After work, he and Susan had gone for a drink. Except for that, he had not seen her except for seven meetings in the park.

When he got back, Susan would be on vacation. She was going to visit her ex-boyfriend in New York.

The sheets on the bed were the color of bricks.

Through the window, he saw a white dog with black ears and black spots lower its haunches to pee. It ran off, chain jingling.

Just before they arrived, apparently, a large German shepherd had killed a small dog in a war over a steak bone. This happened on the front lawn of a house three yards beyond them. The horror of it was still in the air when the two of them drove into the driveway. They both felt that something was wrong, getting out of the car.

Driving to the house, they had listened to the new tapes his wife had bought: Ry Cooder and the sound-track from *Paris, Texas*, a movie that had disturbed her greatly. The Eurythmics. She knew that he liked the Eurythmics.

In the house, his wife had looked down at a large white clam shell filled with pennies. "Do you think this is to test our honesty?" she had said.

What he felt this morning, lying in bed, was sand. Sand had gotten into the bed. Bricks had not begun to crumble.

Susan's ex-boyfriend lived on East Seventh Street. That was three blocks and one avenue away from where his uncle lived.

Usually the car was nosed-in to the high hedge of rose

of Sharon bushes. It was odd not to have a car, however briefly.

He knew the names of bushes and flowers from his wife. There was a rose of Sharon down the road that had been grafted so that it bloomed both pink and lavender. It was an amusing sight at dusk.

They walked. They loved to walk. On the dunes, down the road, where a little sand always blew late in the day, as if an hourglass had tipped over and broken, and the sand had pooled on the counter.

They learned from the natives to keep to the middle of the road at night to avoid skunks.

The roads were kept in good repair. There were ground swells in the winter. Freezing. Thawing. Freezing. Now the roads were smooth and shiny black. They were even smoother than runways.

In a week, he would be flying to Houston on business. His wife might come, and if she did they would drive to Austin to see her sister. People in Texas thought nothing of distance.

It was brighter. Cicadas sent up their rubbing sound. Cars were moving on the main road, although on their street no one had yet started a car.

He had thought about asking the man in the house with pink shutters for a ride to the garage if it was a very hot day. The man was retired; he was always pleasant, and a little lonely, certainly. The drive would take five minutes. He decided not to ask. He had known to begin with that he might say something—that he might just start talking on the way to the garage. This was clear the day he sat outside of Spiritus with the first coffee of the summer.

The man's grandson had visited. A boy seven or eight.

A towhead. He had run into them on the main road and had sat with the boy at the Dairy Queen while his neighbor made a phone call. "What's a turn?" the boy had asked (who knew where they pulled these things out of the air?). He had risen from the bench and turned. He had forgotten the existence of the bird. As the boy talked, he realized that the boy had overhead someone talking about terns. He told the boy the word homonym. The boy's attention wandered to his grandfather in the phone booth. Two teenagers passed, the boy playing grab-ass with the girl.

There were picnic tables in the park across from the skyscraper, though they always sat on a bench.

Well, it was true: he hated even the simplest forms of regimentation.

He had gotten out of the war alive. Do this, do that, don't-think-just-do-it. And by the way: when you really need something, the rules don't apply, so start thinking again if you want to save yourself.

He imagined his wife with him, in the car, in Texas. It would be a rented car. They would listen to the radio— to whatever came on the radio—instead of to music they'd selected.

The summer before, when he dropped the car off at the same garage for some minor repair, it had been returned to him with a Willie Nelson tape in the tape deck. He returned it and the man thanked him profusely. This year the man still remembered him and moved his car to the head of the list.

He did not think he would ever know the man any better than he did now. It would never come to the point where he and the man would have a beer and talk.

A car started.

It was day.

Tuesday.

A dog barked.

His wife shrugged deeper in the bed.

The breeze blew through a snowball bush, so that big flower domes brushed the screen.

None of the screens was torn. The little house was in good repair. It was just odd—a nice, modest house outside, and inside, no thought had been given to fabrics or color; no one cared if patterns clashed or were mismatched, and certainly no one cared whether the colors were seasonal. The house contained whatever had been on sale, obviously. The owners only rented it out. They didn't see the blue-striped pillows that looked like a test pattern, didn't care that the towel that fell from the peg as he brushed against it was a supersized, garish autumn leaf.

The floor was squares of black and white linoleum. His eye went to the mound of pennies in the shell, and he conjured up an image of himself tossing a penny as if it were a rock, raising one leg flamingo-like, hopscotching across the floor.

He thought of the children in the park, playing games. Of Susan, smiling.

After shaving, he left the bathroom and went into the kitchen. He looked at the dishes on the open shelves. He could remember his grandmother telling him that in her day they gave away Depression glass. You got it at the movies: see a movie, get a saucer; see another, get a cup. It came packaged in cereal boxes. She and the other children sailed it back and forth, not caring if they broke the pieces. One of the children in the neighborhood was an awful little boy, and he had such a temper that he'd go outside and sail the plates and cups and saucers into the huge elm tree, and his mother came out, shrieking at him, but that was because of the noise and the mess he was making, not because of the dishes.

He boiled water, took the egg timer from the shelf, tipped it, and lowered an egg into the water. The bubbles rolled like surf. Two minutes passed, during which he fought to forget the taste of mustard on a hot dog, the shock of icy Coke going down his throat, the way the big bank of abelias smelled where the path curved by the fountain, and the smell of Susan's hair—as if, in the city, it had improbably caught a sea breeze.

When the time passed, he cracked the egg into a green glass bowl, put breadsticks on a yellow plate, filled a pink glass with orange juice, and went to surprise his wife with breakfast.

TIMES

It was almost Christmas, and Cammy and Peter were visiting her parents in Cambridge. Late in the afternoon on the second day of their visit, Cammy followed Peter upstairs when he went to take a shower. She wanted a break from trying to make conversation with her mother and father.

"Why is it that I always feel guilty when we're not at my parents' house at Christmas?" he said.

"Call them," she said.

"That makes me feel worse," he said.

He was looking in the mirror and rubbing his chin, though he had shaved just a few hours ago. Every afternoon, she knew, he felt for a trace of beard but didn't shave again if he found it. "They probably don't even notice we're not there," he said. "Who'd have time, with my sister and her *au pair* and her three kids and her cat and her dog and her rabbit."

"Gerbil," Cammy said. She sat at the foot of the bed

while he undressed. Every year was the same; they offered to visit his parents in Kentucky, and his mother hinted that there was not enough room. The year before, he had said that they'd bring sleeping bags. His mother had said that she thought it was silly to have her family sprawled on the floor, and that they should visit at a more convenient time. Several days ago, before Cammy and Peter left New York for Boston, they had got presents in the mail from his parents. Each of them had been sent a Christmas stocking with a fake-fur top. Cammy's stocking contained makeup. Peter's was full of joke presents—a hand buzzer, soap that turned black when you washed your hands, a key chain with a dried yellow fish hanging from it. Peter's stocking had had a hundred-dollar bill folded in the toe. In the toe of her stocking, Cammy found cuticle scissors.

While Peter showered, she wandered around her old room; when they arrived, they had been tired from the long drive, and she went to sleep with no more interest in her surroundings than she would have had in an anonymous motel room. Now she saw that her mother had got rid of most of the junk that used to be here, but she had also added things—her high-school yearbook, a Limoges dish with her Girl Scout ring in it—so that the room looked like a shrine. Years ago, Cammy had rolled little curls of Scotch Tape and stuck them to the backs of pictures of boyfriends or would-be boyfriends and then pushed the snapshots against the mirror to form the shape of a heart. Only two photos remained on the mirror now, both of Michael Grizetti, who had been her steady in her last year of high school. When her mother had moved them and put them neatly under the frame of the mirror, top left and right, she must have discovered the secret. Cammy pulled the larger picture out and turned it over. The hidden snapshot was still glued to the back: Grizzly with his pelvis thrust forward, thumbs pointing at his crotch, and the message "Nil desperandum x x x x x x x x x x" written on the snapshot across his chest. It all seemed so harmless now. He was the first person Cammy had slept with, and most of what she remembered now was what happened after they had sex. They went into New York, with fake IDs and fifty dollars Grizzly borrowed from his brother. She could still remember how the shag carpet tickled the soles of her feet when she went to the window of their hotel in the morning and pulled open the heavy curtains and looked across a distance so short that she thought she could reach out and touch the adjacent building, so close and so high that she couldn't see the sky; there had been no way to tell what kind of day it was. Now she noticed that there was a little haze over Michael Grizetti's top lip in the photograph. It was dust, not a mustache.

Peter came out of the bathroom. Over the years, he had gotten his hair cut closer and closer, so that now when she touched his head the curls were too tight to spring up at her touch. His head looked a little like a cantaloupe—a ridiculous idea, which would be useful just the same; she and her friends always said amusing things about their husbands when they wrote each other. She saved the more flattering images of him as things to say to him after making love. Her high-school English teacher would have approved. The teacher loved to invent little rhymes for the class:

Your conversation can be terrific;
Just remember: be specific

Peter's damp towel flew past her and landed on the bed. As usual, he discarded it as if he had just finished it off in a fight. The week before, he had been in Barbados on a retreat with his company, and he was still very tan. There was a wide band of white skin where he had worn his swiming trunks. In the dim afternoon light he looked like a piece of Marimekko fabric.

He pulled on sweatpants, tied the drawstring, and lit a cigarette with the fancy lighter she had bought him for Christmas. She had given it to him early. It was a metal tube with a piece of rawhide attached to the bottom. When the string was pulled, an outer sleeve of metal rose over the top, to protect the flame. Peter loved it, but she was a little sorry after she gave it to him; there had been something dramatic about huddling in doorways with him, using her body to help him block the wind while he struck matches to light a cigarette. She took two steps toward him now and gave him a hug, putting her hands under his armpits. They were damp. She believed it was a truth that no man ever dried himself thoroughly after showering. He kissed across her forehead, then stopped and pushed his chin between her eyebrows. She couldn't respond; she had told him the night before that she didn't understand how anyone could make love in their parents' house. He shook his head, almost amused, and tucked a thermal shirt into the sweatpants, then pulled on a sweater. "I don't care if it *is* snowing," he said. He was going running.

They walked downstairs. Her father, a retired cardiologist, was on his slant board in the living room, arms raised to heaven, holding the *Wall Street Journal*. "How do you reconcile smoking a pack a day, and then going running?" her father said.

"To tell you the truth," Peter said, "I don't run for my health. It clears my mind. I run because it gives me a high."

"Well, do you think mental health is separate from the health of the body?"

"Oh, Stan," Cammy's mother said, coming into the living room, "no one is trying to argue with you about medicine."

"I wasn't talking about *medicine*," he said.

"People just talk loosely," her mother said.

"I'd never argue that point," her father said.

Cammy found these visits more and more impossible. As a child she had been told what to do and think, and then when she got married her parents had backed off entirely, so that in the first year of her marriage she found herself in the odd position of advising her mother and father. Then, at some point, they had managed to turn the tables again, and now all of them were back to "Go." They argued with each other and made pronouncements instead of having conversations.

She decided to go running with Peter and pulled her parka off a hanger in the closet. She was still having trouble zipping it outside, and Peter helped by pulling the material down tightly in front. It only made her feel more helpless. He saw her expression and nuzzled her hair. "What do you expect from them?" he said, as the zipper went up. She thought, He asks questions he knows I won't bother to answer.

Snow was falling. They were walking through a Christmas-card scene that she hadn't believed in in years; she half expected carolers around the corner. When Peter turned left, she guessed that they were heading for the park on Mass. Avenue. They passed a huge white clapboard house with real candles glowing in all the windows. "Some place," Peter said. "Look at that wreath." The wreath that hung on the front door was so thick that it was convex; it looked as if someone had uprooted a big boxwood and cut a hole in the center. Peter made a snowball and threw it, almost getting a bull's-eye.

"Are you crazy?" she said, grabbing at his hand. "What are you going to do if they open the door?"

"Listen," he said, "if they lived in New York the wreath would be stolen. This way, everybody can enjoy throwing snowballs at it."

On the corner, a man stood staring down at a small brown dog wearing a plaid coat. The blond man standing next to him said, "I told you so. She may be blind, but she still loves it out in the snow." The other man patted the shivering dog, and they continued on their walk.

Christmas in Cambridge. Soon it would be Christmas Eve, time to open the gifts. As usual, she and Peter would be given something practical (stocks), and something frivolous (glasses too fragile for the dishwasher). Then there would be one personal present for each of them: probably a piece of gold jewelry for Cammy and a silk tie for Peter. Cammy occasionally wore one of the ties when she dressed like a nineteen-forties businessman. Peter thought the ties were slightly effeminate—he never liked them. The year before, when her parents gave her a lapis ring, he had pulled it off her finger to examine it on Christmas night, in bed, then pushed it on his little finger and wiggled it, making a Clara Bow mouth and pretending to be gay. He had been trying to show her how ridiculous he would look wearing a wedding ring. They had been married three years then, and some part of her was still so sentimental that she asked him from time to time if he wouldn't reconsider and wear a wedding ring. It wasn't that she thought a ring would be any sort of guarantee. They had lived together for two years before they suddenly decided to get married, but before the wedding they had agreed that it was naive to expect a lifetime of fidelity. If either one became interested in someone else, they would handle the situation in whatever way they felt best, but there would be no flaunting of the other person, and they wouldn't talk about it.

A couple of months before the last trip to her parents'— Christmas a year ago—Peter had waked her up one night to tell her about a young woman he had had a brief affair with. He described his feelings about being with the woman—how much he liked it when she put her hand over his when they sat at a table in a restaurant; the time she had dissipated some anger of his by suddenly putting her lips to the deepening lines in his forehead, to kiss his frown away. Then Peter had wept onto Cammy's pillow. She could still remember his face—the only time she had ever seen him cry—and how red and swollen it was, as if it had been burned. "Is this discreet enough for you?" he had said. "Do you want to push this pillow into my face so not even the *neighbors* can hear?" She didn't care what the neighbors thought, because she didn't even know the neighbors. She had not comforted him or touched the pillow. She had not been dramatic and gone out to sleep on the sofa. After he went to work in the morning, she had several cups of coffee and then went out to try to cheer herself up. She bought flowers at an expensive flower shop on Greenwich Avenue, pointing to individual blossoms for the florist to remove one by one, choosing with great care. Then she went home, trimmed the stems, and put them in little bottles—just a few stalks in each, all flowers and no greens. By evening, when Peter was about to come home, she realized that he would see them and know that she had been depressed, so she bunched them all together again and put them in a vase in the dining room. Looking at them, she suddenly understood how ironic it was that all during the past summer, when she was falling more deeply in love with Peter, he was having a flirtation and then an affair with someone else. Cammy had begun to be comfortable with how subtly attuned to each other they were, and she had been deluded. It made her embarrassed to remember how close she felt to Peter late one fall afternoon on Bleeker Street, when Peter stopped to light a cigarette. Something had made her poke him in the ribs. She didn't often act childish, and she could see that he was taken aback, and that made her laugh and poke him again. Every time he thought she'd finished and tried to light another match, she managed to take him by surprise and tickle him again; she even got through the barrier he'd made with his elbows pointed into his stomach. "What *is* this?" he said. "The American Cancer Society sent you to torture me?" People were looking—who said people don't notice things in New York?—and Peter was backing away, then doubling up, with the cigarette unlit in his mouth, admitting that he couldn't control her. When she moved toward him to hug him and end the game, he didn't believe it was over; he turned sideways, one hand extended to ward her off, clumsily trying to thumb up a flame with his right hand. This was the opposite of the night she had sex with Michael Grizetti: she could remember all of this moment—the smiling fat woman walking by, talking to herself, the buzzing sound of the neon sign outside the restaurant, Peter's stainless-steel watchband sparkling under the street light, the *de-de-de-deeeeeeh* of a car horn in the distance. "Time!" he had shouted, backing away. Then, at a safe distance, he crossed his fingers above his head, like a child.

Now Peter slapped her bottom. "I'm going to run," he said. He took off into the park, his running shoes kicking up clods of snow. She watched him go. He was tall and broad-shouldered, and his short leather jacket came just to his waist, so that he looked like an adolescent in ill-fitting clothes. She had on cowboy boots instead of running shoes. Why did she hold it against him that she had decided at the last minute to go with him and that she was wearing the wrong shoes? Did she expect him to throw down his cape?

She probably would not have thought of a cape at all, except that his scarf flew off as he ran, and he didn't notice. She turned into the park to get it. The snow was falling in smaller flakes now; it was going to stay. Maybe it was the realization that even icier weather was still to come that suddenly made her nearly numb with cold. The desire to be in the sun was almost a hot spot between her ribs; something actually burned inside her. Like everyone she knew, she had grown up watching Porky Pig and Heckle and Jeckle on Saturday mornings—cartoons in which the good guys got what they wanted and no consequences were permanent. Now she wanted one of those small tornadoes that whipped through cartoons, transporting objects and characters with miraculous speed from one place to another. She wanted to believe again in the magic power of the wind.

They went back to the house. Music was playing loudly on the radio, and her father was hollering to her mother, "First we get that damned 'Drummer Boy' dirge, and

now they've got the Andrews Sisters singing 'Boogie
Woogie Bugle Boy.' What the hell does *that* have to do
with Christmas? Isn't that song from the Second World
War? What are they doing playing that stuff at Christmas? Probably some disc jockey that's high. Everybody's
high all the time. The guy who filled my gas tank this
morning was high. The kid they put on to deliver mail's
got eyes like a pinwheel and walks like he might step on
a land mine. What about 'White Christmas'? Do they
think that Bing Crosby spent his whole life playing golf?"

Peter came up behind Cammy as she was hanging his
scarf on a peg on the back of the kitchen door. He
helped her out of her coat and hung it over the scarf.

"Look at this," Cammy's mother said proudly, from
the kitchen.

They walked into the room where her mother stood
and looked down. While they were out, she had finished
making the annual *bûche de Noël*: a fat, perfect cylinder
of a log, with cholocate icing stroked into the texture of
tree bark. A small green-and-white wreath had been
pumped out of a pastry tube to decorate one end, and
there was an open jar of raspberry jam that her mother
must have used to make the bow.

"It was worth my effort," her mother said. "You two
look like children seeing their presents on Christmas
morning."

Cammy smiled. What her mother had just said was
what gave her the idea of touching the Yule log—what
made her grin and begin to wiggle her finger lightly
through a ridge, widening it slightly, giving the bark at
least one imperfection. Once her finger touched it, it
was difficult to stop—though she knew she had to let
the wild upsweep of the tornado she might create stay

an image in her mind. The consolation, naturally, was what would happen when she raised her finger. Slowly— while Peter and her mother stared—she lifted her hand, still smiling, and began to suck the chocolate off her finger.

SUMMER PEOPLE

The first weekend at their summer house in Vermont, Jo, Tom, and Byron went out for pizza. Afterward, Tom decided that he wanted to go dancing at a roadside bar. Byron had come with his father and Jo grudgingly, enthusiastic about the pizza but fearing that it would be a longer night than he wanted. "They have Pac-Man here," Tom said to his son, as he swung the car into the bar parking strip, and for a couple of seconds it was obvious that Byron was debating whether or not to go in with them. "Nah," he said. "I don't want to hang out with a bunch of drunks while you two dance."

Byron had his sleeping bag with him in the car. The sleeping bag and a pile of comic books were his constant companions. He was using the rolled-up bag as a headrest. Now he turned and punched it flatter, making it more a pillow, and then stretched out to emphasize that he wouldn't go in with them.

"Maybe we should just go home," Jo said, as Tom pulled open the door to the bar.

"What for?"

"Byron—"

"Oh, Byron's overindulged," Tom said, putting his hand on her shoulder and pushing her forward with his fingertips.

Byron was Tom's son from his first marriage. It was the second summer that he was spending with them on vacation in Vermont. He'd been allowed to decide, and he had chosen to come with them. In the school year he lived with his mother in Philadelphia. This year he was suddenly square and sturdy, like the Japanese robots he collected—compact, complicated robots, capable of doing useful but frequently unnecessary tasks, like a Swiss Army knife. It was difficult for Tom to realize that his son was ten years old now. The child he conjured up when he closed his eyes at night was always an infant, the tangled hair still as smooth as peach fuzz, with the scars and bruises of summer erased, so that Byron was again a sleek, seal-like baby.

The band's instruments were piled on the stage. Here and there, amps rose out of tangled wire like trees growing from the forest's tangled floor. A pretty young woman with a blond pompadour was on the dance floor, shaking her puff of hair and smiling at her partner, with her Sony earphones clamped on, so that she heard her own music while the band took a break and the jukebox played. The man stood there shuffling, making almost no attempt to dance. Tom recognized them as the couple who had outbid him on a chain saw he wanted at an auction he had gone to earlier in the day.

On the jukebox, Dolly Parton was doing the speaking

part of "I Will Always Love You." Green bottles of Rolling Rock, scattered across the bar top, had the odd configuration of misplaced bowling pins. Dolly Parton's sadness was coupled with great sincerity. The interlude over, she began to sing again, with greater feeling. "I'm not kidding you," a man wearing an orange football jersey said, squeezing the biceps of the burly man who sat next to him. "I says to him, 'I don't understand your question. What is tuna fish *like?* It's tuna fish.' " The burly man's face contorted with laughter.

There was a neon sign behind the bar, with shining bubbles moving through a bottle of Miller. When Tom was with his first wife, back when Byron was about three years old, he had taken the lights off the Christmas tree one year while needles rained down on the bedsheet snowbank they had mounded around the tree stand. He had never seen a tree dry out so fast. He remembered snapping off branches, then going to get a garbage bag to put them in. He snapped off branch after branch, stuffing them inside, feeling clever that he had figured out a way to get the dried-out tree down four flights of stairs without needles dropping everywhere. Byron came out of the back room while this was going on, saw the limbs disappearing into the black bag, and began to cry. His wife never let him forget all the wrong things he had said and done to Byron. He was still not entirely sure what Byron had been upset about that day, but he had made it worse by getting angry and saying that the tree was only a tree, not a member of the family.

The bartender passed by, clutching beer bottles by their necks as if they were birds he had shot. Tom tried to get his eye, but he was gone, involved in some story being told at the far end of the bar. "Let's dance," Tom said, and Jo moved into his arms. They walked to the dance floor and slow-danced to an old Dylan song. The harmonica cut through the air like a party blower, shrilly unrolling.

When they left and went back to the car, Byron pretended to be asleep. If he had really been sleeping, he would have stirred when they opened and closed the car doors. He was lying on his back, eyes squeezed shut a little too tightly, enclosed in the padded blue chrysalis of the sleeping bag.

The next morning, Tom worked in the garden, moving from row to row as he planted tomato seedlings and marigolds. He had a two-month vacation because he was changing jobs, and he was determined to stay ahead of things in the garden this year. It was a very carefully planned bed, more like a well-woven rug than like a vegetable patch. Jo was on the porch, reading *Moll Flanders* and watching him.

He was flattered but also slightly worried that she wanted to make love every night. The month before, on her thirty-fourth birthday, they had drunk a bottle of Dom Pérignon and she had asked him if he was still sure he didn't want to have a child with her. He told her that he didn't, and reminded her that they had agreed on that before they got married. He had thought, from the look on her face, that she was about to argue with him—she was a teacher and she loved debate—but she dropped the subject, saying, "You might change your mind someday." Since then she had begun to tease him. "Change your mind?" she would whisper, curling up next to him on the sofa and unbuttoning his shirt. She even wanted to make love in the living room. He was afraid Byron would wake up and come downstairs for some reason, so he would turn off the television and go upstairs with her. "What *is* this?" he asked once lightly, hoping it wouldn't provoke her into a discussion of whether he had changed his mind about having a child.

"I always feel this way about you," she said. "Do you think I like it the rest of the time, when teaching takes all my energy?"

On another evening, she whispered something else that surprised him—something he didn't want to pursue. She said that it made her feel old to realize that having friends she could stay up all night talking to was a thing of the past. "Do you remember that from college?" she said. "All those people who took themselves so seriously that everything they felt was a fact."

He was glad that she had fallen asleep without really wanting an answer. Byron puzzled him less these days and Jo puzzled him more. He looked up at the sky now: bright blue, with clouds trailing out thinly, so that the ends looked as if kite strings were attached. He was rinsing his hands with the garden hose at the side of the house when a car came up the driveway and coasted to a stop. He turned off the water and shook his hands, walking forward to investigate.

A man in his forties was getting out of the car—clean-cut, pudgy. He reached back into the car for a briefcase, then straightened up. "I'm Ed Rickman!" he called. "How are you today?"

Tom nodded. A salesman, and he was trapped. He wiped his hands on his jeans.

"To get right to the point, there are only two roads in this whole part of the world I really love, and this is one of them," Rickman said. "You're one of the new people—

hell, everybody who didn't crash up against Plymouth
Rock is new in New England, right? I tried to buy this
acreage years ago, and the farmer who owned it wouldn't
sell. Made an offer way back then, when money meant
something, and the man wouldn't sell. You own all these
acres now?"

"Two," Tom said.

"Hell," Ed Rickman said. "You'd be crazy not to be
happy here, right?" He looked over Tom's shoulder.
"Have a garden?" Rickman said.

"Out back," Tom said.

"You'd be crazy not to have a garden," Rickman said.

Rickman walked past Tom and across the lawn. Tom
wanted the visitor to be the one to back off, but Rickman
took his time, squinting and slowly staring about the
place. Tom was reminded of the way so many people pe-
rused box lots at the auction—the cartons they wouldn't
let you root around in because the good things thrown on
top covered a boxful of junk.

"I never knew this place was up for grabs," Rickman
said. "I was given to understand the house and land were
an eight-acre parcel, and not for sale."

"I guess two of them were," Tom said.

Rickman ran his tongue over his teeth a few times.
One of his front teeth was discolored—almost black.

"Get this from the farmer himself?" he said.

"Real-estate agent, three years ago. Advertised in the
paper."

Rickman looked surprised. He looked down at his Top-
Siders. He sighed deeply and looked at the house. "I guess
my timing was bad," he said. "That or a question of style.
These New Englanders are kind of like dogs. Slow to
move. Sniff around before they decide what they think."

He held his briefcase in front of his body. He slapped it a couple of times. It reminded Tom of a beer drinker patting his belly.

"Everything changes," Rickman said. "Not so hard to imagine that one day this'll all be skyscrapers. Condominiums or what have you." He looked at the sky. "Don't worry," he said. "I'm not a developer. I don't even have a card to leave with you in case you ever change your mind. In my experience, the only people who change their minds are women. There was a time when you could state that view without having somebody jump all over you, too."

Rickman held out his hand. Tom shook it.

"Just a lovely place you got here," Rickman said. "Thank you for your time."

"Sure," Tom said.

Rickman walked away, swinging the briefcase. His trousers were too big; they wrinkled across the seat like an opening accordion. When he got to the car, he looked back and smiled. Then he threw the briefcase onto the passenger seat—not a toss but a throw—got in, slammed the door, and drove away.

Tom walked around to the back of the house. On the porch, Jo was still reading. There was a pile of paperbacks on the small wicker stool beside her chair. It made him a little angry to think that she had been happily reading while he had wasted so much time with Ed Rickman.

"Some crazy guy pulled up and wanted to buy the house," he said.

"Tell him we'd sell for a million?" she said.

"I wouldn't," he said.

Jo looked up. He turned and went into the kitchen. Byron had left the top off a jar, and a fly had died in the peanut butter. Tom opened the refrigerator and looked over the possibilities.

Later that same week, Tom discovered that Rickman had been talking to Byron. The boy said he had been walking down the road just then, returning from fishing, when a car rolled up alongside him and a man pointed to the house and asked him if he lived there.

Byron was in a bad mood. He hadn't caught anything. He propped his rod beside the porch door and started into the house, but Tom stopped him. "Then what?" Tom said.

"He had this black tooth," Byron said, tapping his own front tooth. "He said he had a house around here, and a kid my age who needed somebody to hang out with. He asked if he could bring this dumb kid over, and I said no, because I wouldn't be around after today."

Byron sounded so self-assured that Tom did a double take, wondering where Byron was going.

"I don't want to meet some creepy kid," Byron said. "If the guy comes and asks you, say no—O.K.?"

"Then what did he say?"

"Talked about some part of the river where it was good fishing. Where the river curved, or something. It's no big deal. I've met a lot of guys like him."

"What do you mean?" Tom said.

"Guys that talk just to talk," Byron said. "Why are you making a big deal out of it?"

"Byron, the guy's nuts," Tom said. "I don't want you to talk to him anymore. If you see him around here again, run and get me."

"Right," Byron said. "Should I scream, too?"

Tom shivered. The image of Byron screaming frightened him, and for a few seconds he let himself believe that he should call the police. But if he called, what would he say—that someone had asked if his house was for sale and later asked Byron if he'd play with his son?

Tom pulled out a cigarette and lit it. He'd drive across town to see the farmer who'd owned the land, he decided, and find out what he knew about Rickman. He didn't remember exactly how to get to the farmer's house, and he couldn't remember his name. The real-estate agent had pointed out the place, at the top of a hill, the summer he showed Tom the property, so he could call him and find out. But first he was going to make sure that Jo got home safely from the grocery store.

The phone rang, and Byron turned to pick it up.

"Hello?" Byron said. Byron frowned. He avoided Tom's eyes. Then, just when Tom felt sure that it was Rickman, Byron said, "Nothing much." A long pause. "Yeah, sure," he said. "I'm thinking about ornithology."

It was Byron's mother.

The real-estate agent remembered him. Tom told him about Rickman. "*De de de de, De de de de,*" the agent sang—the notes of the theme music from "The Twilight Zone." The agent laughed. He told him the farmer whose land he had bought was named Albright. He didn't have the man's telephone number, but was sure it was in the directory. It was.

Tom got in the car and drove to the farm. A young woman working in a flower garden stood up and held her trowel up like a torch when his car pulled into the drive. Then she looked surprised that he was a stranger. He introduced himself. She said her name. It turned out she was Mr. Albright's niece, who had come with her family to watch the place while her aunt and uncle were in New

Zealand. She didn't know anything about the sale of the land; no, nobody else had come around asking. Tom described Rickman anyway. No, she said, she hadn't seen anyone who looked like that. Over on a side lawn, two Irish setters were barking madly at them. A man—he must have been the woman's husband—was holding them by their collars. The dogs were going wild, and the young woman obviously wanted to end the conversation. Tom didn't think about leaving her his telephone number until it was too late, when he was driving away.

That night, he went to another auction, and when he came back to the car one of the back tires was flat. He opened the trunk to get the spare, glad that he had gone to the auction alone, glad that the field was lit up and people were walking around. A little girl about his son's age came by with her parents. She held a one-armed doll over her head and skipped forward. "I don't feel cheated. Why should you feel cheated? I bought the whole box for two dollars and I got two metal sieves out of it," the woman said to the man. He had on a baseball cap and a black tank top and cutoffs, and sandals with soles that curved at the heel and toe like a canoe. He stalked ahead of the woman, box under one arm, and grabbed his dancing daughter by the elbow. "Watch my dolly!" she screamed, as he pulled her along. "That doll's not worth five cents," the man said. Tom averted his eyes. He was sweating more than he should, going through the easy maneuvers of changing a tire. There was even a breeze.

They floated the tire in a pan of water at the gas station the next morning, looking for the puncture. Nothing was embedded in the tire; whatever had made the hole wasn't there. As one big bubble after another rose to the surface, Tom felt a clutch in his throat, as if he himself might be drowning.

He could think of no good reason to tell the officer at the police barracks why Ed Rickman would have singled him out. Maybe Rickman *had* wanted to build a house on that particular site. The policeman made a fist and rested his mouth against it, his lips in the gully between thumb and finger. Until Tom said that, the policeman had seemed concerned—even a little interested. Then his expression changed. Tom hurried to say that of course he didn't believe that explanation, because something funny was going on. The cop shook his head. Did that mean no, of course not, or no, he did believe it?

Tom described Rickman, mentioning the discolored tooth. The cop wrote this information down on a small white pad. He drew crosshatches on a corner. The cop did not seem quite as certain as Tom that no one could have a grudge against him or anyone in his family. He asked where they lived in New York, where they worked.

When Tom walked out into the sunlight, he felt a little faint. Of course he had understood, even before the cop said it, that there was nothing the police could do at this point. "Frankly," the cop had said, "it's not likely that we're going to be able to keep a good eye out, in that you're on a dead-end road. Not a *route*," the cop said. "Not a *major thoroughfare*." It seemed to be some joke the cop was having with himself.

Driving home, Tom realized that he could give anyone who asked a detailed description of the cop. He had studied every mark on the cop's face—the little scar (chicken pox?) over one eyebrow, the aquiline nose that narrowed

at the tip almost to the shape of a tack. He did not in-
tend to alarm Jo or Byron by telling them where he had
been.

Byron had gone fishing again. Jo wanted to make love
while Byron was out. Tom knew he couldn't.

A week passed. Almost two weeks. He and Jo and
Byron sat in lawn chairs watching the lightning bugs
blink. Byron said he had his eye on one in particular, and
he went *"Beep-beep, beep-beep"* as it blinked. They ate
raw peas Jo had gathered in a bowl. He and Jo had a glass
of wine. The neighbors' M.G. passed by. This summer,
the neighbors sometimes tapped the horn as they passed.
A bird swooped low across the lawn—perhaps a female
cardinal. It was a surprise seeing a bird in the twilight like
that. It dove into the grass, more like a seagull than a
cardinal. It rose up, fluttering, with something in its beak.
Jo put her glass on the little table, smiled, and clapped
softly.

The bird Byron found dead in the morning was a
grackle, not a cardinal. It was lying about ten feet from
the picture window, but until Tom examined the bird's
body carefully, he did not decide that probably it had just
smacked into the glass by accident.

At Rusty's, at the end of summer, Tom ran into the
cop again. They were both carrying white paper bags with
straws sticking out of them. Grease was starting to seep
through the bags. Rickman had never reappeared, and
Tom felt some embarrassment about having gone to see
the cop. He tried not to focus on the tip of the cop's nose.

"Running into a nut like that, I guess it makes getting
back to the city look good," the cop said.

He's thinking *summer people,* Tom decided.

"You have a nice year, now," the cop said. "Tell your wife I sure do envy her her retirement."

"Her retirement?" Tom said.

The cop looked at the blacktop. "I admit, the way you described that guy I thought he might be sent by somebody who had a grudge against you or your wife," he said. "Then at the fire-department picnic I got to talking to your neighbor—that Mrs. Hewett—and I asked her if she'd seen anybody strange poking around before you got there. Hadn't. We got to talking. She said you were in the advertising business, and there was no way of knowing what gripes some lunatic might have with that, if he happened to know. Maybe you walked on somebody's territory, so to speak, and he wanted to get even. And your wife being a schoolteacher, you can't realize how upset some parents get when Johnny doesn't bring home the A's. You never can tell. Mrs. Hewett said she'd been a schoolteacher for a few months herself, before she got married, and she never regretted the day she quit. Said your wife was real happy about her own decision, too." The cop nodded in agreement with this.

Tom tried to hide his surprise. Somehow, the fact that he didn't know that Jo had ever exchanged a word with a neighbor, Karen Hewett, privately made the rest of the story believable. They hardly knew the woman. But why would Jo quit? His credibility with the cop must have been good after all. He could tell from the way the cop studied his face that he realized he had been telling Tom something he didn't know.

When the cop left, Tom sat on the hot front hood of his car, took the hamburgers out of the bag, and ate them. He pulled the straw out of the big container of Coke and took off the plastic top. He drank from the cup, and when the Coke was gone he continued to sit there, sucking ice. Back during the winter, Jo had several times brought up the idea of having a baby, but she hadn't mentioned it for weeks now. He wondered if she had decided to get pregnant in spite of his objections. But even if she had, why would she quit her job before she was sure there was a reason for it?

A teenage girl with short hair and triangle-shaped earrings walked by, averting her eyes as if she knew he'd stare after her. He didn't; only the earrings that caught the light like mirrors interested him. In a convertible facing him, across the lot, a boy and girl were eating their sandwiches in the front seat while a golden retriever in the back moved his head between theirs, looking from left to right and right to left with the regularity of a dummy talking to a ventriloquist. A man holding his toddler's hand walked by and smiled. Another car pulled in, with Hall and Oates going on the radio. The driver turned off the ignition, cutting off the music, and got out. A woman got out the other side. As they walked past, the woman said to the man, "I don't see why we've got to eat exactly at nine, twelve, and six." "Hey, it's twelve-fifteen," the man said. Tom dropped his cup into the paper bag, along with his hamburger wrappers and the napkins he hadn't used. He carried the soggy bag over to the trash can. A few bees lifted slightly higher as he stuffed his trash in. Walking back to the car, he realized that he had absolutely no idea what to do. At some point he would have to ask Jo what was going on.

When he pulled up, Byron was sitting on the front step, cleaning fish over a newspaper. Four trout, one of them very large. Byron had had a good day.

Tom walked through the house but couldn't find Jo.

He held his breath when he opened the closet door; it was unlikely that she would be in there, naked, two days in a row. She liked to play tricks on him.

He came back downstairs, and saw, through the kitchen window, that Jo was sitting outside. A woman was with her. He walked out. Paper plates and beer bottles were on the grass beside their chairs.

"Hi, honey," she said.

"Hi," the woman said. It was Karen Hewett.

"Hi," he said to both of them. He had never seen Karen Hewett up close. She was tanner than he realized. The biggest difference, though, was her hair. When he had seen her, it had always been long and windblown, but today she had it pulled back in a clip.

"Get all your errands done?" Jo said.

It couldn't have been a more ordinary conversation. It couldn't have been a more ordinary summer day.

The night before they closed up the house, Tom and Jo lay stretched out on the bed. Jo was finishing *Tom Jones*. Tom was enjoying the cool breeze coming through the window, thinking that when he was in New York he forgot the Vermont house; at least, he forgot it except for the times he looked up from the street he was on and saw the sky, and its emptiness made him remember stars. It was the sky he loved in the country—the sky more than the house. If he hadn't thought it would seem dramatic, he would have gotten out of bed now and stood at the window for a long time. Earlier in the evening, Jo had asked why he was so moody. He had told her that he didn't feel like leaving. "Then let's stay," she said. It was his opening to say something about her job in the fall. He had hoped she would say something, but he hesitated, and she had only put her arms around him and rubbed her cheek against his chest. All summer, she had seduced him—sometimes with passion, sometimes so subtly he didn't realize what was happening until she put her hand up under his T-shirt or kissed him on the lips.

Now it was the end of August. Jo's sister in Connecticut was graduating from nursing school in Hartford, and Jo had asked Tom to stop there so they could do something with her sister to celebrate. Her sister lived in a one-bedroom apartment, but it would be easy to find a motel. The following day, they would take Byron home to Philadelphia and then backtrack to New York.

In the car the next morning, Tom felt Byron's gaze on his back and wondered if he had overheard their lovemaking the night before. It was very hot by noontime. There was so much haze on the mountains that their peaks were invisible. The mountains gradually sloped until suddenly, before Tom realized it, they were driving on flat highway. Late that afternoon they found a motel. He and Byron swam in the pool, and Jo, although she was just about to see her, talked to her sister for half an hour on the phone.

By the time Jo's sister turned up at the motel, Tom had shaved and showered. Byron was watching television. He wanted to stay in the room and watch the movie instead of having dinner with them. He said he wasn't hungry. Tom insisted that he come and eat dinner. "I can get something out of the machine," Byron said.

"You're not going to eat potato chips for dinner," Tom said. "Get off the bed—come on."

Byron gave Tom a look that was quite similar to the look an outlaw in the movie was giving the sheriff who had just kicked his gun out of reach.

"You didn't stay glued to the set in Vermont all summer and miss those glorious days, did you?" Jo's sister said.

"I fished," Byron said.

"He caught four trout one day," Tom said, spreading his arms and looking from the palm of one hand to the palm of the other.

They all had dinner together in the motel restaurant, and later, while they drank their coffee, Byron dropped quarters into the machine in the corridor, playing game after game of Space Invaders.

Jo and her sister went into the bar next to the restaurant for a nightcap. Tom let them go alone, figuring that they probably wanted some private time together. Byron followed him up to the room and turned on the television. An hour later, Jo and her sister were still in the bar. Tom sat on the balcony. Long before his usual bedtime, Byron turned off the television.

"Good night," Tom called into the room, hoping Byron would call him in.

"Night," Byron said.

Tom sat in silence for a minute. He was out of cigarettes and felt like a beer. He went into the room. Byron was lying in his sleeping bag, unzipped, on top of one of the beds.

"I'm going to drive down to that 7-Eleven," Tom said. "Want me to bring you anything?"

"No, thanks," Byron said.

"Want to come along?"

"No," Byron said.

He picked up the keys to the car and the room key and went out. He wasn't sure whether Byron was still sulking because he had made him go to dinner or whether he

didn't want to go back to his mother's. Perhaps he was
just tired.

Tom bought two Heinekens and a pack of Kools. The
cashier was obviously stoned; he had bloodshot eyes and
he stuffed a wad of napkins into the bag before he pushed
it across the counter to Tom.

Back at the motel, he opened the door quietly. Byron
didn't move. Tom put out one of the two lights Byron
had left on and slid open the glass door to the balcony.

Two people kissed on the pathway outside, passing the
pool on the way to their room. People were talking in the
room below—muted, but it sounded like an argument.
The lights were suddenly turned off at the pool. Tom
pushed his heels against the railing and tipped his chair
back. He could hear the cars on the highway. He felt sad
about something, and realized that he felt quite alone.
He finished a beer and lit a cigarette. Byron hadn't been
very communicative. Of course, he couldn't expect a ten-
year-old boy to throw his arms around him the way he
had when he was a baby. And Jo—in spite of her ardor,
his memory of her, all summer, was of her sitting with
her nose in some eighteenth-century novel. He thought
about all the things they had done in July and August,
trying to convince himself that they had done a lot and
had fun. Dancing a couple of times, auctions, the day on
the borrowed raft, four—no, five—movies, fishing with
Byron, badminton, the fireworks and the sparerib dinner
outside the Town Hall on the Fourth.

Maybe what his ex-wife always said was true: he didn't
connect with people. Jo never said such a thing, though.
And Byron chose to spend the summer with them.

He drank the other beer and felt its effect. It had been
a long drive. Byron probably didn't want to go back to

Philadelphia. He himself wasn't too eager to begin his new job. He suddenly remembered his secretary when he confided in her that he'd gotten the big offer—her surprise, the way she hid her thumbs-up behind the palm of her other hand, in a mock gesture of secrecy. "Where are you going to go from there?" she had said. He'd miss her. She was funny and pretty and enthusiastic—no slouch herself. He'd miss laughing with her, miss being flattered because she thought that he was such a competent character.

He missed Jo. It wasn't because she was off at the bar. If she came back this instant, something would still be missing. He couldn't imagine caring for anyone more than he cared for her, but he wasn't sure that he was still in love with her. He was fiddling, there in the dark. He had reached into the paper bag and begun to wrinkle up little bits of napkin, rolling the paper between thumb and finger so that it formed tiny balls. When he had a palmful, he got up and tossed them over the railing. When he sat down again, he closed his eyes and began what would be months of remembering Vermont: the garden, the neon green of new peas, the lumpy lawn, the pine trees and the smell of them at night—and then suddenly Rickman was there, rumpled and strange, but his presence was only slightly startling. He was just a man who'd dropped in on a summer day. "You'd be crazy not to be happy here," Rickman was saying. All that was quite believable now—the way, when seen in the odd context of a home movie, even the craziest relative can suddenly look amiable.

He wondered if Jo was pregnant. Could that be what she and her sister were talking about all this time in the bar? For a second, he wanted them all to be transformed

into characters in one of those novels she had read all
summer. That way, the uncertainty would end. Henry
Fielding would simply step in and predict the future.
The author could tell him what it would be like, what
would happen, if he had to try, another time, to love
somebody.

The woman who had been arguing with the man was
quiet. Crickets chirped, and a television hummed faintly.
Below him, near the pool, a man who worked at the
motel had rolled a table onto its side. He whistled while
he made an adjustment to the white metal pole that
would hold an umbrella the next day.

CARDS

Sometime during the move from Chicago to New York, just before Josie moved in with Philip Neuveville, she took back her maiden name. I hadn't seen her for a couple of years; when we met again she told me, murmuring as shyly as a young girl asked to dance, that she wasn't Josie Runoff anymore, but Josephine Willoughby.

I've known Josie for nine years, off and on, and it's nice to be in the same city with her again. We often meet for lunch. Today, her pale hair, subtly streaked, touches her shoulders and waves away from her face, making her amber eyes seem larger. No blush on her high cheekbones, pearl earrings, only gloss on her lips. A little tortoiseshell half-moon holds back her bangs. The waiter is impressed. So is the water boy. So are the men at the table to our left. Josie is writing down her recipe for seviche, on the Z page of her book of phone numbers.

She gives the impression that nothing much bothers her—including ripping a page out of her pretty, fabric-covered phone book. She does not look up when the waiter puts down our glasses of Pinot Noir.

"Those men think we're pathetic," I whisper.

"I don't think that's what they're thinking."

"Oh, you think all those boring men have minds swirling like Casanova's. You know what they're thinking about? Getting their son into Dartmouth. Then they're wondering whether they should order a new office chair in black or gray."

"No, they aren't. They're wondering what perfume you have on, and whether you now hate your husband so much because he voted for Reagan that you'd do anything behind his back in the afternoon."

"They're thinking about the big beds at the Helmsley."

"Or the UN Plaza," she says. "And they're feeling very sophisticated because everyone hasn't discovered it. Afterward, they want to go downstairs and swim, right?"

The waiter brings the first course. Josie is having pâté. I'm having borscht, which I'm sure I'll get on my silk blouse. I can already feel the specks of soup flying out of the bowl, like sand in the wind. I stir the sour cream, reluctant to begin.

Josie leans across the table and whispers, "They had money on whether we'd order white wine and arugula salad."

We always eat big lunches. We hate the idea that people might think of us as two ladies who sit around eating broiled sole and frosted grapes. Last week we went to a Greek restaurant for moussaka and lots of bread and butter.

The water boy pours water into my glass.

"I was wrong," she says, buttering a roll. "We do have *Grand Hotel* on tape. Come over Friday and see it. Bring Max."

"He's in Germany."

"Oh, God, why does he travel so much? Philip loves to sit around with Max, and he's never in town. Philip's embarrassed to admit that he misses people. I said that to him, and he drew himself up and said that the only reason he was so interested in Max's whereabouts was because it was clear Max was in the CIA. I thought that CIA hysteria died down years ago. It did with everybody else." She finishes her wine. "What's he doing in Germany?" she says.

One of the four men—the best looking—has turned sideways to listen.

"He's looking over the audit of some company his company does business with."

"You come anyway," she says. "Philip ordered a case of this stuff." She points to her empty glass. The waiter comes to her side and puts down her plate of lamb chops. He moves to my side of the table and puts down my lobster salad. Another waiter asks if we want more wine.

"No, thank you," she says.

The man at the other table crosses his legs. He takes a cigarette out of a silver case and puts it in his mouth. Another man reaches across the table to light it.

"What did Max do about that young woman who was in love with him?"

"I don't know."

"She was calling all the time when you were over there."

"And when I wasn't, I'm sure."

"What did he do?" Josie says, pushing the watercress away from her second lamb chop with her finger.

"I don't know. I'm not even sure the calls have stopped. She started calling him after almost a year."

"I hope I never do that," Josie says.

"That's the perfect opening for me to pretend to be dumb."

"Why? You think it's impossible that I'd do something like that?"

"No. I was just going to say, 'Why would you call Max?'"

"I'll tell you," she says, wiping her mouth, "if you weren't involved with him, I would."

The dishes are cleared away. I order coffee. "Two," Josie says.

Almost instantly, the water boy comes toward the table, cups and saucers held high, steam rising. He puts the coffees on the table, then backs up, waits a second, and goes to get cream and sugar. The man sitting sideways raises his finger for the bill. The steam rising from my coffee comes as high as my chin before it thins and wisps away.

"Philip's CIA craziness," Josie says. "And bringing up marriage just to say that he doesn't see the point of marriage. I could do without either of those routines." She takes another sip of coffee, looks up, and smiles. "Remember the four of us snowed in at your aunt's house in Saratoga? We never thought we'd get out. We had those borrowed skis, and you and I went out until we were bowlegged with pain. I remember that huge picture window she had, with the leather seat cushions. Sitting there with our legs stretched out, looking at the birds flying to the suet ball."

"The kamikaze squirrel."

"Ned liking his tent so much that he went out and pitched it in that blizzard," she says.

Ned and I have been divorced for three years, and I still turn to stone when his name is spoken. I can see how I must appear to others: exaggerated calm, fingers delicately hovering above the rim of the coffee cup, as if I were playing chess. Ned pitching the tent. Ned stalking the squirrel, pointing a broken branch with an alligator-head kitchen mitt on the end. The snow that fell for two days, constantly. Josie was married to Jack Runoff. He loved Beethoven and pretended to love Mozart. The next year they were divorced and he was under indictment for fraud, but the case was dismissed. Ned and Jack had been together in Korea. They considered each other brothers, but Ned couldn't stand classical music. He listened almost exclusively to the Rolling Stones. Once, by pure coincidence, Josie bought Jack a red turtleneck and I bought Ned the same sweater. They got together, and each had on the same thing. Neither ever wore his sweater again.

"I wonder if Ned's still into his wilderness adventures," I say.

"Yeah, he still is," she says, sipping her coffee.

"What do you mean?"

"He still wants to spend every free moment camping. Still talks about the sky as if he just discovered it yesterday."

"How do you know that?" I say.

"Oh, because—oh, why pretend to pass over it? It's the

strangest thing. I didn't look him up, God knows. I went
to the optometrist with Philip. He can't see a thing after
drops are put in his eyes, and he's like a child. I was in
the waiting room, and Ned walked in. He'd scratched his
cornea, riding his bike in Central Park. He'd just moved
to town, and he'd caught a branch in the face. He was
surprised to see me, too. It was awkward. He wasn't sure.
He was looking at me with one eye."

"What did he say?"

"Well, you know, it was awkward. He asked how I
was, and I asked how he was. Then Philip came out, and
right away he started to feel like he was going to faint.
He put his hand out and Ned helped him into a chair.
The nurse went in and got the doctor. Philip was so embarrassed. He's such a child."

"Was he all right?"

"It was only eye drops. They wear off in an hour."

"Ned."

"Oh. Yes. It turned out to be nothing serious. One of
Philip's clients had insisted that his driver bring us over
to the doctor's, so we dropped Ned at his office, too. On
the ride, he and Philip discovered that they both passed
up working on the same account. They got together after
that and had lunch. Philip had him over to dinner. I
thought we'd see him once, and that would be that."

"Did he bring somebody to dinner?"

"Well, of course he did. You've been divorced for
years, haven't you?" She sighs. "We just see them every
couple of weeks."

"You see him every two weeks? How long—?"

"I didn't want to talk about it and depress you," she
says. "I felt awkward, though. As though I were doing

something sneaky." She brushes her hair off her shoulder. "He's Philip's friend, not mine."

"If you want me to be magnanimous and say that there's no reason why he shouldn't be your friend, I can't do that. I don't think he should be your friend."

"He isn't. They go up to Philip's brother's place in Maine. I don't go."

"What do you do?" I say.

"Well, what do you think I do? Sleep with him?"

"I didn't say that. And it's rather insulting—"

"Oh, don't say 'rather,' " she says, reaching across the table and clasping my wrist. "I can't tell Philip whom to have for a friend and whom not to have."

"You do remember how crazy he was," I say.

"He wasn't crazy, he was mean."

"He's not anymore?"

"He's pleasant. I'm pleasant. What do you think I should do?"

"I'm sorry," I say.

"You don't have any reason to apologize. It's awkward. To tell the truth, the real problem is that I won't stand up to Philip. I just said that Ned was somebody I'd known slightly years ago, because I could tell right away that he liked him. He always says I don't like anybody he likes. So I'm trying to be nice. I'm trying to convince him that he should marry me."

"He should."

"He should, but no matter what a good little girl I am, he won't. He would have married me before this if he'd decided to do it."

"He loves you, though," I say.

"Yes," she says. "And Max loves you."

Our hands are folded on the table. The waiter moves slowly into Josie's peripheral vision. She turns toward him, reaching for the bill.

"It's mine," I say.

"I know it's tacky to fight over checks," she says, taking the check from the waiter, "but I feel so awful. Let me treat you to lunch."

"What do you have to feel awful about?"

"Having said anything at all. But you know—if you found out, you'd think I was a traitor or something. It was just one of those bizarre things."

She unzips her handbag one-handed, clamping it against her with her elbow. "If it will make you feel better, thank you," I say.

"Good," she says.

The waiter takes the tray. His pants legs are slightly different lengths; they're rolled at the cuff, not sewn. He is wearing orthopedic shoes. He takes the check from our table and from the men's table. He hurries across the room and comes back, bowing as he puts the little tray back on the table. He goes to the other table. The water boy is there, pouring water.

I'm reaching for my shoulder bag when the man at the next table says, "Josephine Runoff." Josie and I both snap our heads around. The man is smiling. "I don't know what your credit line is, so I'm afraid I'll have to return this," he says.

By mistake, the waiter has put Josie's card on the man's tray. He holds it out, but sees that she can't reach it. Both start to rise. His white napkin falls on the floor. He walks to our table, smiling.

"Thank you," she says.

He lifts his card off our tray. "The bills are right," he says. "Just mixed up the cards."

"You may be sorry," she says. "My line of credit is excellent."

"And so is the food here," he says. "Have you eaten here before?"

"Often," Josie says.

"Good restaurant," he says again. "We've started coming here just about every other day."

We both smile. Subtle, but the message has registered: this is the place to find him.

The waiter, seeing us talking, suspects his error and hurries to the table.

"It's fine," the man says. "A problem easily solved. I was sure I wasn't Josephine Runoff."

We get our coats. I leave a dollar in the big brass bowl. The maitre d' opens the door. Outside, the street is dotted with bright-yellow taxis. People moving in all directions. A nurse passes by, pushing a stroller. A messenger zigs and zags through honking traffic, pedaling the bicycle with no hands.

"Get the feeling that that man's not going to forget your name?" I say. Josie and I are walking close together in the wind.

"It won't do him any good," she says. "I'm not Josephine Runoff. I'm Josephine Willoughby, who wants to be Ms. Willoughby-Neuveville." She shakes her head. "Isn't it all silly?" she says. "Being this age and wanting so much to change? Waiting isn't one of my virtues. Not so long ago, I would have flirted. Let a few days pass, then gone back there for lunch. We would have gone to—where did you say? The Helmsley."

"Would you really have done that?"

"Probably," she says. She smiles. She reaches in her pocket, takes something out, and holds it in front of us.

"Back at the office, full of hope," she sighs.

"His business card?" I say, reaching for it. "The man in the restaurant?"

"Of course you realize that he asked the waiter to make the mistake," she says.

"When did he give you this?" I say. "Why didn't you tell me?"

"I am telling you. He palmed it to me underneath my American Express card." She takes it back, drops it in her pocket again, and links arms with me. "That excites men, doesn't it?" she says. "Pulling off something sneaky and acting blasé." She's looking at the sidewalk, and I see her smile before the wind whips her hair across her face. "They just don't know," she says. "We do it all the time."

HEAVEN
ON A
SUMMER NIGHT

Will stood in the kitchen doorway. He seemed to Mrs. Camp to be a little tipsy. It was a hot night, but that alone wouldn't account for his shirt, which was not only rumpled but hanging outside his shorts. Pens, a pack of cigarettes, and what looked like the tip of a handkerchief protruded from the breast pocket. Will tapped his fingertips on the pens. Perhaps he was not tapping them nervously but touching them because they were there, the way Mrs. Camp's mother used to run her fingers over the rosary beads she always kept in her apron pocket. Will asked Mrs. Camp if she would cut the lemon pound cake she had baked for the morning. She thought that the best thing to do when a person had had too much to drink was to humor him, so she did. Everyone had little weaknesses, to be sure, but Will and his sister had grown up to be good people. She had known them since they were toddlers, back when she had first come to work for the Wildes here in Charlottesville. Will was her favorite, then and now, although Kate probably loved her more. Will was nineteen now, and Kate twenty. On the wall, above the sink, was a framed poem that Kate had written and illustrated when she was in the fifth grade:

Like is a cookie
Love is a cake

Like is a puddle
Love is a lake

Years later, Will told her that Kate hadn't made up the poem at all. It was something she had learned in school.

Mrs. Camp turned toward Will, who was sitting at the table. "When does school start?" she said.

"There's a fly!" he said, dropping the slice of cake back onto his plate.

"What?" Mrs. Camp said. She had been at the sink, rinsing glasses before loading them into the dishwasher. She left the water running. The steam rose and thinned out as it floated toward the ceiling. "It's a raisin," she said. "You got me all worried about a raisin."

He plucked some more raisins out of the pound cake and then took another bite.

"If you don't want to talk about school, that's one thing, but that doesn't mean you should holler out that there's a fly in the food," Mrs. Camp said.

A year ago, Will had almost flunked out of college, in his sophomore year. His father had talked to the dean by long distance, and Will was allowed to continue. Now, in the summer, Mr. Wilde had hired Will a tutor in mathematics. Mornings and early afternoons, when Will was not being tutored or doing math problems, he painted houses with his friend Anthony Scoresso. Scoreboard and Will were going to drive to Martha's Vineyard to paint a house there at the end of August. The house was unoccupied, and although she was a little hesitant about doing such a thing, Mrs. Camp was going to accept Will's invitation to go with the boys and stay in the house for the week they were painting it. Scoreboard loved her cooking. She had never been to the Vineyard.

Now that they were older, Will and Kate included Mrs. Camp in many things. They had always told her everything. That was the difference between being who she was and being a parent—they knew that they could tell her anything. She never met one of their friends without hearing what Will or Kate called the Truth. That handsome blond boy, Neal, who told the long story about hitchhiking to the West Coast, Will told her later, was such a great storyteller because he was on speed. The girl called Natasha who got the grant to study in Italy had actually been married *and* divorced when she was eighteen, and her parents never even knew it. Rita, whom Mrs. Camp had known since first grade, now slept with a man as old as her father, for money. It pleased Kate and Will when a worried look came over Mrs. Camp's face as she heard these stories. Years ago, when she told them once that she liked that old song by the Beatles, "Lucy in the Sky with Diamonds," Will announced gleefully that the Beatles were singing about a drug.

Kate's car pulled into the driveway as Mrs. Camp was rinsing the last of the dishes. Kate drove a little white Toyota that made a gentle sound, like rain, as the tires rolled over the gravel. Will got up and pulled open the screen door for his sister on his way to the liquor cabinet. He poured some gin into a glass and walked to the refrigerator and added tonic water but no ice. In this sort of situation, Mrs. Camp's mother would have advised keeping quiet and saying a prayer. Mrs. Camp's husband—he was off on a fishing trip on the Chesapeake somewhere— would never advise her to pray, of course. Lately, if she asked him for advice about almost anything, his reply was "Get off my back." She noticed that Will noticed that she was looking at him. He grinned at her and put down his drink so that he could tuck in his shirt. As he raised the shirt, she had a glimpse of his long, tan back and thought of the times she had held him naked as a baby— all the times she had bathed him, all the hours she had held the hose on him in the backyard. Nowadays, he and Scoreboard sometimes stopped by the house at lunchtime. With their sun-browned bodies flecked with paint, they sat at the table on the porch in their skimpy shorts, waiting for her to bring them lunch. They hardly wore any more clothes than Will had worn as a baby.

Kate came into the kitchen and dropped her canvas tote bag on the counter. She had been away to see her boyfriend. Mrs. Camp knew that men were always going to fascinate Kate, the way her tropical fish had fascinated her many summers earlier. Mrs. Camp felt that most men moved in slow motion, and that that was what attracted women. It hypnotized them. This was not the way men at work were. On the job, construction workers sat up straight and drove tractors over piles of dirt and banged through potholes big enough to sink a bicycle, but at home, where the women she knew most often saw their men, they spent their time stretched out in big chairs, or standing by barbecue grills, languidly turning a hamburger as the meat charred.

Kate had circles under her eyes. Her long brown hair was pulled back into a bun at the nape of her neck. She had spent the weekend, as she had every weekend this summer, with her boyfriend, Frank Crane, at his condominium at Ocean City. He was studying for the bar exam. Mrs. Camp asked Kate how his studying was going, but Kate simply shook her head impatiently. Will, at the refrigerator, found a lime and held it up for them to see, very pleased. He cut off a side, squeezed lime juice into his drink, then put the lime back in the refrigerator, cut side down, on top of the butter-box lid. He hated to wrap anything in wax paper: Mrs. Camp knew that.

"Frank did the strangest thing last night," Kate said, sitting down and slipping her feet out of her sandals. "Maybe it wasn't strange. Maybe I shouldn't say."

"That'll be the day," Will said.

"What happened?" Mrs. Camp said. She thought that Frank was too moody and self-absorbed, and she thought that this was another story that was going to prove her right. Kate looked sulky—or maybe just more tired than Mrs. Camp had noticed at first. Mrs. Camp took a bottle of soda water out of the refrigerator and put it on the table, along with the lime and a knife. She put two glasses on the table and sat down across from Kate. "Perrier?" she said. Kate and Will liked her to call everything by its proper name, unless they had given it a nickname themselves. Secretly, she thought of it as bubble water.

"I was in his bedroom last night, reading, with the sheet pulled up," Kate said. "His bathroom is across the hall from the bedroom. He went to take a shower, and

when he came out of the bathroom I turned back the
sheet on his side of the bed. He just stood there, in the
doorway. We'd had a kind of fight about that friend of
his, Zack. The three of us had gone out to dinner that
night, and Zack kept giving the waitress a hard time
about nothing. Sassing a waitress because a dab of ice
cream was on the saucer when she brought it. Frank knew
I was disgusted. Before he took his shower, he went into
a big thing about how I wasn't responsible for his friends'
actions, and said that if Zack had acted as bad as I said
he did he'd only embarrassed himself."

"If Frank passes the bar exam this time around, you
won't have anything to worry about," Will said. "He'll
act nice again."

Kate poured a glass of Perrier. "I haven't told the story
yet," she said.

"Oh," Will said.

"I thought everything between us was fine. When he
stopped in the doorway, I put the magazine down and
smiled. Then he said, 'Kate—will you do something for
me?' " Kate looked at Mrs. Camp, then dropped her eyes.
"We were going to bed, you know," she said. "I thought
things would be better after a while." Kate looked up.
Mrs. Camp nodded and looked down. "Anyway," Kate
went on, "he looked so serious. He said, 'Will you do
something for me?' and I said, 'Sure. What?' and he said,
'I just don't know. Can you think of something to cheer
me up?' "

Will was sipping his drink, and he spilled a little
when he started laughing. Kate frowned.

"You take everything so seriously," Will said. "He was
being funny."

"No, he wasn't," Kate said softly.

"What did you do?" Mrs. Camp said.

"He came over to the bed and sat down, finally. I knew he felt awful about something. I thought he'd tell me what was the matter. When he didn't say anything, I hugged him. Then I told him a story. I can't imagine what possessed me. I told him about Daddy teaching me to drive. How he was afraid to be in the passenger seat with me at the wheel, so he pretended I needed practice getting into the garage. Remember how he stood in the driveway and made me pull in and pull out and pull in again? I never had any trouble getting into the garage in the first place." She took another sip of Perrier. "I don't know what made me tell him that," she said.

"He was kidding. You said something funny, too, and that was that," Will said.

Kate got up and put her glass in the sink. It was clear, when she spoke again, that she was talking only to Mrs. Camp. "Then I rubbed his shoulders," she said. "Actually, I only rubbed them for a minute, and then I rubbed the top of his head. He likes to have his head rubbed, but he gets embarrassed if I start out there."

Kate had gone upstairs to bed. *Serpico* was on television, and Mrs. Camp watched with Will for a while, then decided that it was time for her to go home. Here it was August 25th already, and if she started addressing Christmas cards tonight she would have a four-month jump on Christmas. She always bought cards the day after Christmas and put them away for the following year.

Mrs. Camp's car was a 1977 Volvo station wagon. Mr. and Mrs. Wilde had given it to her in May, for her birthday. She loved it. It was the newest car she had ever driven. It was dark, shiny green—a color only velvet could be, the color she imagined Robin Hood's jacket must have been. Mr. Wilde had told her that he was not leaving her anything when he died but that he wanted to be nice to her when he was aboveground. A strange way to put it. Mrs. Wilde gave her a dozen pink Depression-glass wine goblets at the same time they gave her the car. There wasn't one nick in any of the rims; the glasses were all as smooth as sea-washed stones.

As she drove, Mrs. Camp wondered if Will had been serious when he said to Kate that Frank was joking. She was sure that Will slept with girls. (Will was not there to rephrase her thoughts. He always referred to young girls as women.) He must have understood that general anxiety or dread Frank had been feeling, and he must also have known that having sex wouldn't diminish it. It was also possible that Will was only trying to appear uninterested because Kate's frank talk embarrassed him. "Frank talk" was a pun. Those children had taught her so much. She still felt a little sorry that they had always had to go to stuffy schools that gave them too much homework. She even felt sorry that they had missed the best days of television by being born too late: no "Omnibus," no "My Little Margie," no "Our Miss Brooks." The reruns of "I Love Lucy" meant nothing to them. They thought Eddie Fisher's loud tenor voice was funny, and shook their heads in disbelief when Lawrence Welk, looking away from the camera, told folks how nice the song was that had just been sung. Will and Kate had always found so many things absurd and funny. As children, they were as united in their giggling as they were now in their harsh dismissals of people they didn't care for. But maybe this gave them an advantage over someone like her mother, who always held her tongue, because laughter allowed them to dismiss things; the things were forgotten by the time they ran out of breath.

In the living room, Mr. Camp was asleep in front of the television. *Serpico* was on. She didn't remember the movie exactly, but she would be surprised if Al Pacino ever got out of his dilemma. She dropped her handbag in a chair and looked at her husband. It was the first time she had seen him in almost two weeks. Since his brother retired from the government and moved to a house on the Chesapeake, Mr. Camp hardly came home at all. Tonight, many cigarettes had been stubbed out in the ashtray on the table beside his chair. He had on blue Bermuda shorts and a lighter blue knit shirt, white socks, and tennis shoes. His feet were splayed on the footstool. When they were young, he had told her that the world was theirs, and, considering the world her mother envisioned for her—the convent—he'd been right. He had taught her, all in one summer, how to drive, smoke, and have sex. Later, he taught her how to crack crabs and how to dance a rumba.

It was eight o'clock, and outside the light was as blue-gray as fish scales. She went into the kitchen, tiptoeing. She went to the refrigerator and opened the door to the freezer. She knew what she would find, and of course it was there: bluefish, foil-wrapped, neatly stacked to within an inch of the top of the freezer. He had made room for all of them by removing the spaghetti sauce. She closed the door and pulled open the refrigerator door. There were the two containers. The next night, she would make up a big batch of spaghetti. The night after that, they would start eating the fish he'd caught. She opened the freezer door and looked again. The shining rectangles rose up like steep silver steps. The white air blowing off the ice, surrounding them and drifting out, made her squint. It might have been clouds, billowing through heaven. If she could shrink to a fraction of her size, she could walk into the cold, close the door, and start to climb.

She was tired. It was as simple as that. This life she loved so much had been lived, all along, with the greatest effort. She closed the door again. To hold herself still, she held her breath.

WHERE
YOU'LL FIND
ME

Friends keep calling my broken arm a broken wing. It's the left arm, now folded against my chest and kept in place with a blue scarf sling that is knotted behind my neck, and it weighs too much ever to have been winglike. The accident happened when I ran for a bus. I tried to stop it from pulling away by shaking my shopping bags like maracas in the air, and that's when I slipped on the ice and went down.

So I took the train from New York City to Saratoga yesterday, instead of driving. I had the perfect excuse not to go to Saratoga to visit my brother at all, but once I had geared up for it I decided to go through with the trip and avoid guilt. It isn't Howard I mind but his wife's two children—a girl of eleven and a boy of three. Becky either pays no attention to her brother Todd or else she tortures him. Last winter she used to taunt him by stalking around the house on his heels, clomping close behind him wherever he went, which made him run and scream at the same time. Kate did not intervene until both children became hysterical and we could no longer shout over their voices. "I think I like it that they're physical," she said. "Maybe if they enact some of their hostility like this, they won't grow up with the habit of getting what they want by playing mind games with other people." It seems to me that they will not ever grow up but will burn out like meteors.

Howard has finally found what he wants: the opposite of domestic tranquility. For six years, he lived in Oregon with a pale, passive woman. On the rebound, he married an even paler pre-med student named Francine. That marriage lasted less than a year, and then, on a blind date in Los Angeles, he met Kate, whose husband was away on a business trip to Denmark just then. In no time, Kate and her daughter and infant son moved in with him, to the studio apartment in Laguna Beach he was sharing with a screenwriter. The two men had been working on a script about Medgar Evers, but when Kate and the children moved in they switched to writing a screenplay about what happens when a man meets a married woman with two children on a blind date and the three of them move in with him and his friend. Then Howard's collaborator got engaged and moved out, and the screenplay was abandoned. Howard accepted a last-minute invitation to teach writing at an upstate college in New York, and within a week they were all ensconced in a drafty Victorian house in Saratoga. Kate's husband had begun divorce proceedings before she moved in with Howard, but eventually he agreed not to sue for custody of Becky and Todd in exchange for child-support payments that were less than half of what his lawyer thought he would have to pay. Now he sends the children enormous stuffed animals that they have little or no interest in, with notes that say, "Put this in Mom's zoo." A stuffed toy every month or so—giraffes, a life-size German shepherd, an overstuffed standing bear—and, every time, the same note.

The bear stands in one corner of the kitchen, and people have gotten in the habit of pinning notes to it—reminders to buy milk or get the oil changed in the car. Wraparound sunglasses have been added. Scarves and jackets are sometimes draped on its arms. Sometimes the stuffed German shepherd is brought over and propped up with its paws placed on the bear's haunch, imploring it.

Right now, I'm in the kitchen with the bear. I've just turned up the thermostat—the first one up in the morning is supposed to do that—and am dunking a tea bag in a mug of hot water. For some reason, it's impossible for me to make tea with loose tea and the tea ball unless I have help. The only tea bag I could find was Emperor's Choice.

I sit in one of the kitchen chairs to drink the tea. The chair seems to stick to me, even though I have on thermal long johns and a long flannel nightgown. The chairs are plastic, very nineteen-fifties, patterned with shapes that look sometimes geometric, sometimes almost human. Little things like malformed hands reach out toward triangles and squares. I asked. Howard and Kate got the kitchen set at an auction, for thirty dollars. They thought it was funny. The house itself is not funny. It has four fireplaces, wide-board floors, and high, dusty ceilings. They bought it with his share of an inheritance that came to us when our grandfather died. Kate's contribution to restoring the house has been transforming the baseboards into faux marbre. How effective this is has to do with how stoned she is when she starts. Sometimes the baseboards look like clotted versions of the kitchen-chair pattern, instead of marble. Kate considers what she calls "parenting" to be a full-time job. When they first moved to Saratoga, she used to give piano lessons. Now she ignores the children and paints the baseboards.

And who am I to stand in judgment? I am a thirty-eight-year-old woman, out of a job, on tenuous enough footing with her sometime lover that she can imagine crashing emotionally as easily as she did on the ice. It may be true, as my lover, Frank, says, that having money is not good for the soul. Money that is given to you, that is. He is a lawyer who also has money, but it is money he earned and parlayed into more money by investing in real estate. An herb farm is part of this real estate. Boxes of herbs keep turning up at Frank's office—herbs in foil, herbs in plastic bags, dried herbs wrapped in cones of newspaper. He crumbles them over omelets, roasts, vegetables. He is opposed to salt. He insists herbs are more healthful.

And who am I to claim to love a man when I am skeptical even about his use of herbs? I am embarrassed to be unemployed. I am insecure enough to stay with someone because of the look that sometimes comes into his eyes when he makes love to me. I am a person who secretly shakes on salt in the kitchen, then comes out with her plate, smiling, as basil is crumbled over the tomatoes.

Sometimes, in our bed, his fingers smell of rosemary or tarragon. Strong smells. Sour smells. Whatever Shakespeare says, or whatever is written in *Culpeper's Complete Herbal*, I cannot imagine that herbs have anything to do with love. But many brides-to-be come to the herb farm and buy branches of herbs to stick in their bouquets. They anoint their wrists with herbal extracts, to smell mysterious. They believe that herbs bring them luck. These days, they want tubs of rosemary in their houses, not ficus trees. "I got in right on the cusp of the new world," Frank says. He isn't kidding.

For the Christmas party tonight, there are cherry tomatoes halved and stuffed with peaks of cheese, mushrooms stuffed with puréed tomatoes, tomatoes stuffed with chopped mushrooms, and mushrooms stuffed with cheese. Kate is laughing in the kitchen. "No one's going to notice," she mutters. "No one's going to say anything."

"Why don't we put out some nuts?" Howard says.

"Nuts are so conventional. This is funny," Kate says, squirting more soft cheese out of a pastry tube.

"Last year we had mistletoe and mulled cider."

"Last year we lost our sense of humor. What happened that we got all hyped up? We even ran out on Christmas Eve to cut a tree—"

"The kids," Howard says.

"That's right," she says. "The kids were crying. They were feeling competitive with the other kids, or something."

"Becky was crying. Todd was too young to cry about that," Howard says.

"Why are we talking about tears?" Kate says. "We can talk about tears when it's not the season to be jolly. Everybody's going to come in tonight and love the wreaths on the picture hooks and think this food is so *festive*."

"We invited a new Indian guy from the Philosophy Department," Howard says. "American Indian—not an Indian from India."

"If we want, we can watch the tapes of 'Jewel in the Crown,' " Kate says.

"I'm feeling really depressed," Howard says, backing up to the counter and sliding down until he rests on his elbows. His tennis shoes are wet. He never takes off his wet shoes, and he never gets colds.

"Try one of those mushrooms," Kate says. "They'll be better when they're cooked, though."

"What's wrong with me?" Howard says. It's almost the first time he's looked at me since I arrived. I've been trying not to register my boredom and my frustration with Kate's prattle.

"Maybe we should get a tree," I say.

"I don't think it's Christmas that's making me feel this way," Howard says.

"Well, snap out of it," Kate says. "You can open one of your presents early, if you want to."

"No, no," Howard says, "it isn't Christmas." He hands a plate to Kate, who has begun to stack the dishwasher. "I've been worrying that you're in a lot of pain and you just aren't saying so," he says to me.

"It's just uncomfortable," I say.

"I know, but do you keep going over what happened, in your mind? When you fell, or in the emergency room, or anything?"

"I had a dream last night about the ballerinas at Victoria Pool," I say. "It was like Victoria Pool was a stage set instead of a real place, and tall, thin ballerinas kept parading in and twirling and pirouetting. I was envying their being able to touch their fingertips together over their heads."

Howard opens the top level of the dishwasher and Kate begins to hand him the rinsed glasses.

"You just told a little story," Howard says. "You didn't really answer the question."

"I don't keep going over it in my mind," I say.

"So you're repressing it," he says.

"Mom," Becky says, walking into the kitchen, "is it O.K. if Deirdre comes to the party tonight if her dad doesn't drive here to pick her up this weekend?"

"I thought her father was in the hospital," Kate says.

"Yeah, he was. But he got out. He called and said that it was going to snow up north, though, so he wasn't sure if he could come."

"Of course she can come," Kate says.

"And you know what?" Becky says.

"Say hello to people when you come into a room," Kate says. "At least make eye contact or smile or something."

"I'm not Miss America on the runway, Mom. I'm just walking into the kitchen."

"You have to acknowledge people's existence," Kate says. "Haven't we talked about this?"

"Oh, hel-*lo*," Becky says, curtsying by pulling out the sides of an imaginary skirt. She has on purple sweatpants. She turns toward me and pulls the fabric away from her hipbones. "Oh, hello, as if we've never met," she says.

"Your aunt here doesn't want to be in the middle of this," Howard says. "She's got enough trouble."

"Get back on track," Kate says to Becky. "What did you want to say to me?"

"You know what you do, Mom?" Becky says. "You make an issue of something and then it's like when I speak it's a big thing. Everybody's listening to me."

Kate closes the door to the dishwasher.

"Did you want to speak to me privately?" she says.

"Nooo," Becky says, sitting in the chair across from me and sighing. "I was just going to say—and now it's a big deal—I was going to say that Deirdre just found out that that guy she was writing all year is in *prison*. He was in prison all the time, but she didn't know what the P.O. box meant."

"What's she going to do?" Howard says.

"She's going to write and ask him all about prison," Becky says.

"That's good," Howard says. "That cheers me up to hear that. The guy probably agonized about whether to tell her or not. He probably thought she'd hot-potato him."

"Lots of decent people go to prison," Becky says.

"That's ridiculous," Kate says. "You can't generalize about convicts any more than you can generalize about the rest of humanity."

"So?" Becky says. "If somebody in the rest of humanity had something to hide, he'd hide it, too, wouldn't he?"

"Let's go get a tree," Howard says. "We'll get a tree."

"Somebody got hit on the highway carrying a tree home," Becky says. "Really."

"You really do have your ear to the ground in this town," Kate says. "You kids could be the town crier. I know everything before the paper comes."

"It happened yesterday," Becky says.

"Christ," Howard says. "We're talking about crying, we're talking about death." He is leaning against the counter again.

"We are not," Kate says, walking in front of him to open the refrigerator door. She puts a plate of stuffed tomatoes inside. "In your typical fashion, you've singled out two observations out of a lot that have been made, and—"

"I woke up thinking about Dennis Bidou last night," Howard says to me. "Remember Dennis Bidou, who used to taunt you? Dad put me up to having it out with him, and he backed down after that. But I was always afraid he'd come after me. I went around for years pretending not to cringe when he came near me. And then, you know, one time I was out on a date and we ran out of gas, and as I was walking to get a can of gas a car pulled up alongside me and Dennis Bidou leaned out the window. He was surprised that it was me and I was surprised that it was him. He asked me what happened and I said I ran out of gas. He said, 'Tough shit, I guess,' but a girl was driving and she gave him a hard time. She stopped the car and insisted that I get in the back and they'd take me to the gas station. He didn't say one word to me the whole way there. I remembered the way he looked in the car when I found out he was killed in Nam—the back of his head on that ramrod-straight body, and a black collar or some dark-colored collar pulled up to his hairline." Howard makes a horizontal motion with four fingers, thumb folded under, in the air beside his ear.

"Now you're trying to depress everybody," Kate says.

"I'm willing to cheer up. I'm going to cheer up before tonight. I'm going up to that Lions Club lot on Main Street and get a tree. Anybody coming with me?"

"I'm going over to Deirdre's," Becky says.

"I'll come with you, if you think my advice is needed," I say.

"For fun," Howard says, bouncing on his toes. "For fun—not advice."

He gets my red winter coat out of the closet, and I
back into it, putting in my good arm. Then he takes a
diaper pin off the lapel and pins the other side of the coat
to the top of my shoulder, easing the pin through my
sweater. Then he puts Kate's poncho over my head. This
is the system, because I am always cold. Actually, Kate
devised the system. I stand there while Howard puts on
his leather jacket. I feel like a bird with a cloth draped
over its cage for the night. This makes me feel sorry for
myself, and then I *do* think of my arm as a broken wing,
and suddenly everything seems so sad that I feel my eyes
well up with tears. I sniff a couple of times. And Howard
faced down Dennis Bidou, for my sake! My brother! But
he really did it because my father told him to. Whatever
my father told him to do he did. He drew the line only
at smothering my father in the hospital when he asked
him to. That is the only time I know of that he ignored
my father's wishes.

"Get one that's tall enough," Kate says. "And don't
get one of those trees that look like a cactus. Get one
with long needles that swoops."

"Swoops?" Howard says, turning in the hallway.

"Something with some fluidity," she says, bending her
knees and making a sweeping motion with her arm. "You
know—something beautiful."

Before the guests arrive, a neighbor woman has brought
Todd back from his play group and he is ready for bed,
and the tree has been decorated with a few dozen Christmas balls and some stars cut out of typing paper, with
paper-clip hangers stuck through one point. The smaller
animals in the stuffed-toy menagerie—certainly not the
bear—are under the tree, approximating the animals at

the manger. The manger is a roasting pan, with a green dinosaur inside.

"How many of these people who're coming do I know?" I say.

"You know . . . you know . . ." Howard is gnawing his lip. He takes another sip of wine, looks puzzled. "Well, you know Koenig," he says. "Koenig got married. You'll like his wife. They're coming separately, because he's coming straight from work. You know the Miners. You know—you'll really like Lightfoot, the new guy in the Philosophy Department. Don't rush to tell him that you're tied up with somebody. He's a nice guy, and he deserves a chance."

"I don't think I'm tied up with anybody," I say.

"Have a drink—you'll feel better," Howard says. "Honest to God. I was getting depressed this afternoon. When the light starts to sink so early, I never can figure out what I'm responding to. I gray over, like the afternoon, you know?"

"O.K., I'll have a drink," I say.

"The very fat man who's coming is in A.A.," Howard says, taking a glass off the bookshelf and pouring some wine into it. "These were just washed yesterday," he says. He hands me the glass of wine. "The fat guy's name is Dwight Kule. The Jansons, who are also coming, introduced us to him. He's a bachelor. Used to live in the Apple. Mystery man. Nobody knows. He's got a computer terminal in his house that's hooked up to some mysterious office in New York. Tells funny jokes. They come at him all day over the computer."

"Who are the Jansons?"

"You met her. The woman whose lover broke into the house and did caricatures of her and her husband all over

the walls after she broke off with him. One amazing
artist, from what I heard. You know about that, right?"
"No," I say, smiling. "What does she look like?"
"You met her at the races with us. Tall. Red hair."
"Oh, that woman. Why didn't you say so?"
"I told you about the lover, right?"
"I didn't know she had a lover."
"Well, fortunately she *had* told her husband, and
they'd decided to patch it up, so when they came home
and saw the walls—I mean, I get the idea that it was
rather graphic. Not like stumbling upon hieroglyphics in
a cave or something. Husband told it as a story on him-
self: going down to the paint store and buying the darkest
can of blue paint they had to do the painting-over, because he wanted it done with—none of this three-coats
stuff." Howard has another sip of wine. "You haven't
met her husband," he says. "He's an anesthesiologist."
"What did her lover do?"
"He ran the music store. He left town."
"Where did he go?"
"Montpelier."
"How do you find all this stuff out?"
"Ask. Get told," Howard says. "Then he was cleaning
his gun in Montpelier the other day, and it went off and
he shot himself in the foot. Didn't do any real damage,
though."
"It's hard to think of anything like that as poetic justice," I say. "So are the Jansons happy again?"
"I don't know. We don't see much of them," Howard
says. "We're not really involved in any social whirl, you
know. You only visit during the holidays, and that's when
we give the annual party."
"Oh, hel-*lo*," Becky says, sweeping into the living room

from the front door, bringing the cold and her girlfriend Deirdre in with her. Deirdre is giggling, head averted. "My friends! My wonderful friends!" Becky says, trotting past, hand waving madly. She stops in the doorway, and Deirdre collides with her. Deirdre puts her hand up to her mouth to muffle a yelp, then bolts past Becky into the kitchen.

"I can remember being that age," I say.

"I don't think I was ever that stupid," Howard says.

"A different thing happens with girls. Boys don't talk to each other all the time in quite the same intense way, do they? I mean, I can remember when it seemed that I never talked but that I was always *confiding* something."

"Confide something in me," Howard says, coming back from flipping the Bach on the stereo.

"Girls just talk that way to other girls," I say, realizing he's serious.

"Gidon Kremer," Howard says, clamping his hand over his heart. "God—tell me that isn't beautiful."

"How did you find out so much about classical music?" I say. "By asking and getting told?"

"In New York," he says. "Before I moved here. Before L.A., even. I just started buying records and asking around. Half the city is an unofficial guide to classical music. You can find out a lot in New York." He pours more wine into his glass. "Come on," he says. "Confide something in me."

In the kitchen, one of the girls turns on the radio, and rock and roll, played low, crosses paths with Bach's violin. The music goes lower still. Deirdre and Becky are laughing.

I take a drink, sigh, and nod at Howard. "When I was in San Francisco last June to see my friend Susan, I got in a night before I said I would, and she wasn't in town," I say. "I was going to surprise her, and she was the one who surprised me. It was no big deal. I was tired from the flight and by the time I got there I was happy to have the excuse to check into a hotel, because if she'd been there we'd have talked all night. Acting like Becky with Deirdre, right?"

Howard rolls his eyes and nods.

"So I went to a hotel and checked in and took a bath, and suddenly I got my second wind and I thought what the hell, why not go to the restaurant right next to the hotel—or in the hotel, I guess it was—and have a great dinner, since it was supposed to be such a great place."

"What restaurant?"

"L'Étoile."

"Yeah," he says. "What happened?"

"I'm telling you what happened. You have to be patient. Girls always know to be patient with other girls."

He nods yes again.

"They were very nice to me. It was about three-quarters full. They put me at a table, and the minute I sat down I looked up and there was a man on a banquette across the room from me. He was looking at me, and I was looking at him, and it was almost impossible not to keep eye contact. It just hit both of us, obviously. And almost on the other side of the curve of the banquette was a woman, who wasn't terribly attractive. She had on a wedding ring. He didn't. They were eating in silence. I had to force myself to look somewhere else, but when I did look up he'd look up, or he'd already be looking up. At some point he left the table. I saw that in my peripheral vision, when I had my head turned to hear a conversation on my right and I was chewing my food. Then after a while he paid the check and the two of them left. She walked ahead of him, and he didn't seem to be with her. I mean, he walked quite far behind her. But naturally he didn't turn his head. And after they left I thought, That's amazing. It was really like kinetic energy. Just wham. So I had coffee, and then I paid my check, and when I was leaving I was walking up the steep steps to the street and the waiter came up behind me and said, 'Excuse me. I don't know what I should do, but I didn't want to embarrass you in the restaurant. The gentleman left this for you on his way out.' And he handed me an envelope. I was pretty taken aback, but I just said, 'Thank you,' and continued up the steps, and when I got outside I looked around. He wasn't there, naturally. So I opened the envelope, and his business card was inside. He was one of the partners in a law firm. And underneath his name he had written, 'Who are you? Please call.'"

Howard is smiling.

"So I put it in my purse and I walked for a few blocks, and I thought, Well, what for, really? Some man in San Francisco? For what? A one-night stand? I went back to the hotel, and when I walked in the man behind the desk stood up and said, 'Excuse me. Were you just eating dinner?,' and I said, 'A few minutes ago,' and he said, 'Someone left this for you.' It was a hotel envelope. In the elevator on the way to my room, I opened it, and it was the same business card, with 'Please call' written on it."

"I hope you called," Howard says.

"I decided to sleep on it. And in the morning I decided not to. But I kept the card. And then at the end of August I was walking in the East Village, and a couple obviously from out of town were walking in front of me, and a punk kid got up off the stoop where he was sitting and said to them, 'Hey—I want my picture taken with you.' I went into a store, and when I came out the couple and the punk kid were all laughing together, holding these Polaroid snaps that another punk had taken. It was a joke, not a scam. The man gave the kid a dollar for one of the pictures, and they walked off, and the punk sat back down on the stoop. So I walked back to where he was sitting, and I said, 'Could you do me a real favor? Could I have my picture taken with you, too?' "

"What?" Howard says. The violin is soaring. He gets up and turns the music down a notch. He looks over his shoulder. "Yeah?" he says.

"The kid wanted to know why I wanted it, and I told him because it would upset my boyfriend. So he said yeah—his face lit up when I said that—but that he really would appreciate two bucks for more film. So I gave it to him, and then he put his arm around me and really mugged for the camera. He was like a human boa constrictor around my neck, and he did a Mick Jagger pout. I couldn't believe how well the picture came out. And that night, on the white part on the bottom I wrote, 'I'm somebody whose name you still don't know. Are you going to find me?' and I put it in an envelope and mailed it to him in San Francisco. I don't know why I did it. I mean, it doesn't seem like something I'd ever do, you know?"

"But how will he find you?" Howard says.

"I've still got his card," I say, shrugging my good shoulder toward my purse on the floor.

"You don't know what you're going to do?" Howard says.

"I haven't thought about it in months."

"How is that possible?"

"How is it possible that somebody can go into a restaurant and be hit by lightning and the other person is, too? It's like a bad movie or something."

"Of course it can happen," Howard says. "Seriously, what are you going to do?"

"Let some time pass. Maybe send him something he can follow up on if he still wants to."

"That's an amazing story," Howard says.

"Sometimes—well, I hadn't thought about it in a while, but at the end of summer, after I mailed the picture, I'd be walking along or doing whatever I was doing and this feeling would come over me that he was thinking about me."

Howard looks at me strangely. "He probably was," he says. "He doesn't know how to get in touch with you."

"You used to be a screenwriter. What should he do?"

"Couldn't he figure out from the background that it was the Village?"

"I'm not sure."

"If he could, he could put an ad in the Voice."

"I think it was just a car in the background."

"Then you've got to give him something else," Howard says.

"For what? You want your sister to have a one-night stand?"

"You make him sound awfully attractive," Howard says.

"Yeah, but what if he's a rat? It could be argued that he was just cocky, and that he was pretty sure that I'd respond. Don't you think?"

"I think you should get in touch with him. Do it in some amusing way if you want, but I wouldn't let him slip away."

"I never had him. And from the looks of it he has a wife."

"You don't know that."

"No," I say. "I guess I don't know."

"Do it," Howard says. "I think you need this," and when he speaks he whispers—just what a girl would do. He nods his head yes. "Do it," he whispers again. Then he turns his head abruptly, to see what I am staring at. It is Kate, wrapped in a towel after her bath, trailing the long cord of the extension phone with her.

"It's Frank," she whispers, her hand over the mouthpiece. "He says he's going to come to the party after all."

I look at her dumbly, surprised. I'd almost forgotten that Frank knew I was here. He's only been here once with me, and it was clear that he didn't like Howard and Kate. Why would he suddenly decide to come to the party?

She shrugs, hand still over the mouthpiece. "Come here," she whispers.

I get up and start toward the phone. "If it's not an awful imposition," she says, "maybe he could bring Deirdre's father with him. He lives just around the corner from you in the city."

"Deirdre's father?" I say.

"Here," she whispers. "He'll hang up."

"Hi, Frank," I say, talking into the phone. My voice sounds high, false.

"I miss you," Frank says. "I've got to get out of the city. I invited myself. I assume since it's an annual invitation it's all right, right?"

"Oh, of course," I say. "Can you just hold on for one second?"

"Sure," he says.

I cover the mouthpiece again. Kate is still standing next to me.

"I was talking to Deirdre's mother in the bathroom," Kate whispers. "She says that her ex-husband's not really able to drive yet, and that Deirdre has been crying all day. If he could just give him a lift, they could take the train back, but—"

"Frank? This is sort of crazy, and I don't quite understand the logistics, but I'm going to put Kate on. We need for you to do us a favor."

"Anything," he says. "As long as it's not about Mrs. Joan Wilde-Younge's revision of a revision of a revision of a spiteful will."

I hand the phone to Kate. "Frank?" she says. "You're about to make a new friend. Be very nice to him, because he just had his gallbladder out, and he's got about as much strength as seaweed. He lives on Seventy-ninth Street."

I am in the car with Howard, huddled in my coat and the poncho. We are on what seems like an ironic mission. We are going to the 7-Eleven to get ice. The moon is shining brightly, and patches of snow shine like stepping stones in the field on my side of the car. Howard puts on his directional signal suddenly and turns, and I look over my shoulder to make sure we're not going to be hit from behind.

"Sorry," he says. "My mind was wandering. Not that it's the best-marked road to begin with."

Miles Davis is on the tape deck—the very quiet kind of Miles Davis.

"We've got a second for a detour," he says.

"Why are we detouring?"

"Just for a second," Howard says.

"It's freezing," I say, dropping my chin to speak the words so my throat will warm up for a second. I raise my head. My clavicle is colder.

"What you said about kinetic energy made me think about doing this," Howard says. "You can confide in me and I can confide in you, right?"

"What are you talking about?"

"This," he says, turning onto property marked "No Trespassing." The road is quite rutted where he turns onto it, but as it begins to weave up the hill it smooths out a little. He is driving with both hands gripping the wheel hard, sitting forward in the seat as if the extra inch, plus the brights, will help him see more clearly. The road levels off, and to our right is a pond. It is not frozen, but ice clings to the sides, like scum in an aquarium. Howard clicks out the tape, and we sit there in the cold and silence. He turns off the ignition.

"There was a dog here last week," he says.

I look at him.

"Lots of dogs in the country, right?" he says.

"What are we doing here?" I say, drawing up my knees.

"I fell in love with somebody," he says.

I had been looking at the water, but when he spoke I turned and looked at him again.

"I didn't think she'd be here," he says quietly. "I didn't even really think that the dog would be here. I just felt drawn to the place, I guess—that's all. I wanted to

see if I could get some of that feeling back if I came here.
You'd get it back if you called that man, or wrote him.
It was real. I could tell when you were talking to me that
it was real."

"Howard, did you say that you fell in love with somebody? When?"

"A few weeks ago. The semester's over. She's graduating. She's gone in January. A graduate student—like that?
A twenty-two-year-old kid. One of my pal Lightfoot's
philosophy students." Howard lets go of the wheel.
When he turned the ignition off, he had continued to
grip the wheel. Now his hands are on his thighs. We both
seem to be examining his hands. At least, I am looking at
his hands so I do not stare into his face, and he has
dropped his eyes.

"It was all pretty crazy," he says. "There was so much
passion, so fast. Maybe I'm kidding myself, but I don't
think I let on to her how much I cared. She saw that I
cared, but she . . . she didn't know my heart kept stop-
ping, you know? We drove out here one day and had a
picnic in the car—it would have been your nightmare
picnic, it was so cold—and a dog came wandering up to
the car. Big dog. Right over there."

I look out my window, almost expecting that the dog
may still be there.

"There were three freezing picnics. This dog turned up
at the last one. She liked the dog—it looked like a mutt,
with maybe a lot of golden retriever mixed in. I thought
it was inviting trouble for us to open the car door, because it didn't look like a particularly friendly dog. But
she was right and I was wrong. Her name is Robin, by
the way. The minute she opened the door, the dog
wagged its tail. We took a walk with it." He juts his chin

forward. "Up that path there," he says. "We threw rocks
for it. A sure crowd-pleaser with your average lost-in-the-
woods American dog, right? I started kidding around,
calling the dog Spot. When we were back at the car,
Robin patted its head and closed the car door, and it
backed off, looking very sad. Like we were really ruining
its day, to leave. As I was pulling out, she rolled down
the window and said, 'Goodbye, Rover,' and I swear its
face came alive. I think his name really was Rover."

"What did you do?" I say.

"You mean about the dog, or about the two of us?"

I shake my head. I don't know which I mean.

"I backed out, and the dog let us go. It just stood
there. I got to look at it in the rearview mirror until the
road dipped and it was out of sight. Robin didn't look
back."

"What are you going to do?"

"Get ice," he says, starting the ignition. "But that isn't
what you meant, either, is it?"

He backs up, and as we swing around toward our own
tire tracks I turn my head again, but there is no dog
there, watching us in the moonlight.

Back at the house, as Howard goes in front of me up
the flagstone pathway, I walk slower than I usually do in
the cold, trying to give myself time to puzzle out what
he makes me think of just then. It comes to me at the
moment when my attention is diverted by a patch of ice
I'm terrified of slipping on. He reminds me of that court-
house figure—I don't know what it's called—the statue of
a blindfolded woman holding the scales of justice. Bag
of ice in the left hand, bag of ice in the right—but there's
no blindfold. The door is suddenly opened, and what

Howard and I see before us is Koenig, his customary bandanna tied around his head, smiling welcome, and behind him, in the glare of the already begun party, the woman with red hair holding Todd, who clutches his green dinosaur in one hand and rubs his sleepy, crying face with the other. Todd makes a lunge—not really toward his father but toward wider spaces—and I'm conscious, all at once, of the cigarette smoke swirling and of the heat of the house, there in the entranceway, that turn the bitter-cold outdoor air silver as it comes flooding in. "Messiah"—Kate's choice of perfect music for the occasion—isn't playing; someone has put on Judy Garland, and we walk in just as she is singing, "That's where you'll find me." The words hang in the air like smoke.

"Hello, hello, hello, hello," Becky calls, dangling one kneesocked leg over the balcony as Deirdre covers her face and hides behind her. "To both of you, just because you're here, from me to you: a million—a trillion—hellos."

ABOUT THE AUTHOR

Ann Beattie was born in Washington, D.C., and was educated at American University and the University of Connecticut. She has taught at the University of Virginia and Harvard. She is the author of three novels, *Chilly Scenes of Winter*, *Falling in Place*, and *Love Always*; and three collections of stories, *Distortions*, *Secrets and Surprises*, and *The Burning House*. Ms. Beattie lives in Charlottesville, Virginia.